NOCTURNE

FRANK SWINNERTON wa[...] an impoverished family, a[...] hood in the poorer area[...] Holloway, Finsbury Park, [...] In 1901 he joined J. M. [...] tionist, and in 1907 became a publisher's reader at Chatto & Windus, where he was eventually to become an editor.

He was prolific as both a novelist and critic. His first novel, *The Merry Heart*, was published in 1909, and subsequent novels include *Harvest Comedy* (1937) and *A Tigress in Prothero* (1959). Critical studies of George Gissing and Robert Louis Stevenson appeared in 1912 and 1914 respectively. He also contributed critical pieces to *Truth and Nation*, the *Evening News*, and the *Observer*, and his last critical work, *Arnold Bennett: A Last Word*, was published in 1978 when he was ninety-four.

He was President of the Royal Literary Fund 1962–66 and remained a familiar literary figure until his death in 1982.

BENNY GREEN has been a jazz musician and jazz critic, as well as a literary, film, and television critic. He is well-known as a journalist and broadcaster. His most recent publications include *Shaw's Companions*, *Fred Astaire*, and *P. G. Wodehouse*. He is also a cricket enthusiast and is the editor of the *Wisden Anthology*.

ALSO AVAILABLE IN

TWENTIETH-CENTURY CLASSICS

FRANK SWINNERTON
Nocturne

—«‹◊›»—

INTRODUCED BY
BENNY GREEN

Oxford   New York
OXFORD UNIVERSITY PRESS
1986

Oxford University Press, Walton Street, Oxford OX2 6DP

Oxford New York Toronto
Delhi Bombay Calcutta Madras Karachi
Kuala Lumpur Singapore Hong Kong Tokyo
Nairobi Dar es Salaam Cape Town
Melbourne Auckland

and associated companies in
Beirut Berlin Ibadan Nicosia

Oxford is a trade mark of Oxford University Press

Introduction © Benny Green 1985

First published 1917 by Martin Secker Ltd.
First issued, with Benny Green's Introduction, as an
Oxford University Press paperback 1986

British Library Cataloguing in Publication Data

Swinnerton, Frank
Nocturne. —(Twentieth-century classics)
I. Title II.Series
823'.912[F] PR6037.W85
ISBN 0-19-281947-X

Library of Congress Cataloging in Publication Data

Swinnerton, Frank, 1884–
Nocturne.
(Twentieth-century classics)
I. Title. II. Series.
PR6037.W85N6 1986 823'.912 85-29686
ISBN 0-19-281947-X (pbk.)

Printed in Great Britain by
The Guernsey Press Co. Ltd.
Guernsey, Channel Islands

CONTENTS

INTRODUCTION

BY BENNY GREEN

The genesis of few novels have been more minutely documented, or become more widely known, than that of the book which the reader now holds in his hand. We know the specific social occasion on which its possibilities were first discussed, we know who was present and who said what. We know how the title came about, and which fellow-authors suggested alternatives. We know where and when precisely the book was written, the structural rules which governed its composition, the pace at which it was written, the method by which it was despatched to the printers, the size of the first print order, the tempo at which it first sold. We know also that its first real success came in America, and we know why and at whose instigation. We know what all sorts of famous writers thought of it, and, most priceless of all, what the man responsible for it thought of it, much to the embarrassment, I should imagine, of those who had been boosting it so vociferously over so long a period. We know what its British sales were in 1920, 1921, 1922 and so on. The candour of its author has enlightened us regarding its errors and misuse of words, and even gone so far as

suggesting to us that the inclusion of one
section of the book was clumsy error.

And yet, for all our detailed knowledge of its
career, *Nocturne* remains one of the most
readable and durable books of its day, a
beautifully balanced example of something
extremely rare in English literature, a story of
working-class life told from within the palisades
of the working class. Frank Swinnerton once
rejected this judgement, but the rejection was
couched in such a way, and placed in such a
context, as to confirm rather than refute the
argument. In *Autobiography*, he writes 'I have
never drawn characters direct from life, and
all the people, male and female, in my novels
are imaginary'. He then adds, with that
scrupulosity which in all his critical writings
about himself becomes a comic weapon. 'It
occurs to me that this is not quite true, but it
is nearly true'. Elsewhere in his auto-
biography, Swinnerton describes how as a
child his family often went hungry, moved
from one slum to the next, spent long years of
shabby-genteel privation until at last he and his
brothers and sisters grew up and slowly eased
the load on their widowed mother. Yet he says
of his family, 'They regarded themselves as
being altogether outside class; they were
craftsmen, ironists, characters, but not
politicians'. In the sense that all artists are
declassé, Swinnerton is perfectly in order, but

in the economic sense, his experience of childhood in Clerkenwell, in Holloway, where 'the vermin walked upon my face at night and woke me', in Finsbury Park and at East Finchley, gave him an insight into the workaday routine of the lower orders without which the subtleties of *Nocturne* could never have been achieved. The action of the book takes place in south London, across the great divide of the Thames, and again Swinnerton is at pains to disabuse us of autobiographical intent. Writing of himself in the third person he says:

his imagination turned at once to the kind of people he had known as a child. He had no acquaintance with any such girls as Jenny and Emmy; they and their companions in the book were as fictitious as the story. His only familiarity with Kennington Park was gained by some walks taken in that neighbourhood while the book was in progress. His life had been spent entirely in districts north of the Thames, where it is believed that Northerners are superior to Southrons. But essential experience of mean streets was at his command.

As a rebuttal of the autobiographical theory this statement is so contradictory that the reader begins to wonder if even Swinnerton himself quite understood his own creative methods. For all the romancing about 'village London' indulged in by literary sociologists who have come by their metropolitan theories

at some provincial university, the back streets
of the poor are much of a muchness whether in
Kennington Park or in the Holloway Road, or
in Finsbury Park or in any of the other
verminous dormitories occupied by the lower
nine-tenths. *Nocturne* was necessarily a book
written in a great hurry. There was no time for
agonizing, or elaborate plot-making. In racing
against the clock Swinnerton understandably
returned to the heartlands of his own
experience, fashioning a strangely pathetic tale
out of the recollections, if not of people, then of
types of people, encountered in childhood.

It becomes necessary to explain the nature of
Swinnerton's tearing hurry while writing
Nocturne. In 1901, then aged fifteen, he had
joined the publishing house of J. M. Dent as
receptionist, clerk and general dogsbody. After
six years of Dent's curmudgeonly dictatorship,
he moved on to Chatto and Windus, where he
grew into an aspiring novelist and a trusted
reader of manuscripts. By the time the Great
War began he was associated with the then still
unproven young publisher Martin Secker, was
the author of several modestly praised but
resolutely uncommercial novels, and was
beginning to amass an encyclopaedic range of
knowledge about the book business. One day
in 1916 Swinnerton lunched with Secker and
an employee of Heinemanns called Nigel de
Grey, who began telling his two friends about

a novelist of his acquaintance who could not think of a theme for his next book. de Gray then said, 'I didnt suggest it to him, but I wonder nobody has ever written a novel about the doings of a single night'. Both Secker and Swinnerton seemed at first surprised that no such novel existed, but later, as the pair of them were walking back to the office, Swinnerton was, as he later put it, 'struck by an impulse', and, turning to Secker, he said, 'How would you like me to write a book about the events of a single night?'. Secker accepted the offer and Swinnerton set to work, reassured only by the knowledge that whatever the obstacles before him, length would not be one of the, for his current contract to write novels for Methuen left him free to write fiction for other publishers but only at short length.

Swinnerton was now 32 years old with an invalid mother to care for. In his auto-biography he lists the chores to be completed each day before the writing of the book could proceed: prepare and eat lunch, feed mother, read manuscripts from the office, write reports, make supper, put hot-water bottles against frozen pipes, clear table, wash dishes, and then at eight oclock in the evening, settle down to write for two hours. At ten oclock he would go to his mother's bedroom and read her the night's work. Always she would fall asleep before he reached the end. He stuck to this routine for a fortnight, then had a failure of nerve which lasted the same length of time. Then he continued for another fortnight and completed the story. As each chapter was finished he posted it to Secker. On the day after sending off the final chapter he received the galley proofs of the first chapter. Secker's reaction to the first parcel was 'I think it opens well', to the second 'I think it's very good', to the third 'I think it's a masterpiece'. Swinnerton, who, I suspect, agreed with the first judgement, was prepared to accept the second, and had a quiet chuckle over the third, was meanwhile preoccupied with the problem of what to call the book. His first plan was to borrow from one of his favourite poems, by Herrick, and entitled it *Night Piece*. This idea was abandoned because such a title was 'orally ambiguous', although even its ambiguity was a vast improvement on the original working title, *The Black Cloak*. At this point Swinnerton's uncanny knack of inspiring the solicitude of his fellow-writers took a hand. First there was Raphael Sabatini, who offered him the title *Nocturne*. But Arnold Bennett, who had befriended Swinnerton some time before and had quickly realised that if this mild-mannered young man would not lift a finger in his own cause, then his friends must lift it for him, insisted that the book be called *In the Night*, even though he had not read the book nor even met its publisher. Bennett was adamant: 'You must call the book *In the Night*. You'll sell it in thousands'.

In those days Bennett's worldly wisdom regarding the tides of publishing fortune was generally considered to be infallible, and so Secker, remarking to Swinnerton, 'Oh, let's sell it in thousands', decided that *In the Night* it must be. At which point a certain Lord Gorell, evidently unaware that he was frustrating the cause of the fine arts, suddenly published a book called *In the Night*, thus pre-empting Bennett's dream of vast sales. Sabatini's suggestion, *Nocturne*, now succeeded by default. When the book appeared critical attitudes were fairly hostile, but thanks to the intervention of yet another of Swinnerton's benevolent literary uncles, H. G. Wells, who evangelised shamelessly on the book's behalf, the first editon of 1500 copies gradually sold out. *Nocturne* then fell out of print for a year and was eventually reprinted only because of 'a small but persistent demand'. What made it into a celebrated book was its remarkable American fortunes. Unbeknown to Swinnerton, his agent, the ubiquitous J. B. Pinker, had conspired with George Doran to boost the book in America by persuading Wells to contribute a preface. The upshot is described by Swinnerton as 'a furore':

The Wells preface, and a personal sketch supplied by Arnold Bennett, made the book's fortune in the United States quite extraordinary. There *Nocturne* sold ten thousand copies within a few weeks of publication, and it has continued to sell ever since. It was praised to the skies. The noise was so great that reports of it crossed the Atlantic, and the only book of mine which caused my vigilant mother to fall asleep, made me for a time really famous. From 1918 to 1934 the sales of *Nocturne* were about a thousand copies a year. In America I think very nearly 50,000 copies have been sold. The book has been widely translated, first into Dutch (with adorable annotations, such as that which explains the English word 'stew' as 'een soort stamppot met gestoofd vleesch'), then into Swedish, French, Italian, Czech, and even, I understand, Russian. It has broken the hearts of half a dozen dramatists who though they saw in its brevity and form the makings of a play, and it is the only novel of mine to stir the quidnuncs. But as for me, I must confess that I think nothing of it. The very quality which so many cleverish people have admired—its conception in terms of a time-table—is to me a cause of discomfort. Normally I begin with a situation or with characters; and whatever the defects of this method it is at least imaginatively pure. *Nocturne*, though as a work of imagination it is sincere enough, began with artificiality and is the only stunt book I ever wrote. I detest stunts.

Discounting for the moment Swinnerton's astonishing self-effacement and candour regarding his own writing, we can find several clues to the nature of the book under discussion, especially the references to a time-table and to brevity. Swinnerton's contract with Methuen gave him freedom to publish novels elsewhere provided the full text was less than 80,000 words; *Nocturne* runs to almost exactly 50,000. As to the time-table, we know from the conversations with Secker and de Grey that Swinnerton was restricting himself to the events of a few hours in the lives of a few people. There are the two sisters, Jenny and Emmy, two young men involved in their lives, Alf and Keith, and, unwittingly inhibiting the actions of the girls, their invalid father, who requires constant nursing. One or other of the girls must always be with their father. On the night of Swinnerton's story, both girls catch what they take to be a glimpse of freedom. Only one of them can follow up that glimpse. Which is to be? Which of the two young men is the more worthy? And, as the central issue of the story, which of the two sisters, the domestic drudge Emmy or the self-centred dreamer Jenny, is the more admirable human being? Pervading the lives of these people, struggling to keep their heads above a poverty line, is a set or recurring symbols; Westminster Bridge, water, darkness, food, boats.

On the face of it this list is surprising. Swinnerton's nautical experience was more or less nil. Yet his account of how the heroine boards 'The Minerva', the disposition of the cabin, the close detail into which he goes when describing the furniture, are all so convincing that we get the feeling that the writer has been himself inside this cabin. And so he had. In April 1913, Arnold Bennett, determined as ever to taste the pleasures of comparitive opulence, saw a Dutch yacht called 'The Velsa', lying anchored in the Thames off Richmond. Soon it was his, and he quickly fell into the habit of inviting close friends to share its amenities. 'The Velsa' was a modest enough affair, and by no means the only incident in Bennett's seagoing life. During the Great War he lent it to the Admiralty, and in 1916, before Swinnerton had so much as dreamed of writing a book about the events of a single night, had sold her. But Swinnerton had been much impressed by 'The Velsa' and now saw it as a possible solution to one of the trickiest technical problems facing him in telling his story of Londoners living in grinding poverty of a kind which may all too easily ruin the romantic effect:

I saw Westminster Bridge at night, a picture which always had a singular effect upon my nerves. Then, although instantly possessed of the three chief characters, I hesitated over the background for one emotional exchange. A cramped room smelling of supper would cheapen this; a bedroom was impossible. I thought about the problem for days.

As if by fate, I suddenly caught sight on my bookshelves of a copy of Arnold Bennett's *The Grand Babylon Hotel*. I recalled the weekend I had spent on Bennett's yacht 'The Velsa', just before the outbreak of war. Bennett, to my terror, had rowed me at night in a dinghy over deep silent water to the pier or jetty at Holehaven; and memory of this was so powerful that I shuddered. Everything became clear.

As the yacht was Bennett's, he took a proprietory command over all nautical aspects of *Nocturne*, and was quick to correct Swinnerton where he had erred. No Yacht would lie at anchor in the Thames at Westminster Bridge; it would be moored. Jenny was far too experienced a milliner to wear a hat so soon after having steamed it into what Swinnerton defines as 'revived jauntiness'. And, carrying pedantry almost into the realms of moonshine, Swinnerton apologises to posterity for having implied that Keith might be deprived of a share of his father's estate; Keith, being a Scotsman, could never be subjected to that indignity.

As to the book's structure, Swinnerton was his customary meticulous self. The division of his story into three sections, 'Evening', 'Night' and 'Morning' seems so efficacious that the reader is inclined not to notice that in fact we never reach morning at all, but take our leave of the characters still in the darkness of the small hours. But within each of the three

section, Swinnerton breaks up his story into a
succession of duologues. Apart from the occasional mumbled intercession of Pa, virtually
the entire novel consists of exchanges between
pairs of characters: Jenny and Em, Jenny and
Keith, Jenny and Alf, Em and Alf, Jenny and
Em. Again Swinnerton was merciless with
himself. Acknowledging that a good case could
be made to prove that the section 'After the
Theatre' comprises the best piece of writing in
the book, he is nonetheless insistent that its
inclusion breaches the symmetry of his structure. After all, says Swinnerton, *Nocturne* is
supposed to be the story of Jenny, who never
appears in 'After the Theatre'. Yet the reader
is all too ready to forgive this hypothetical
breach of the structural proprieties for the
sheer pleasure of enjoying the delicacy and
sureness of touch with which Swinnerton
describes the sudden dramatic flowering of
romance between stolid, inhibited Em and
clumsy, embarrassed Alf. In the technical
sense, this is the high point of the book's
achievement, for what Swinnerton has to do
is to show with a reasonable degree of
verisimiltude the behaviour of a pair of
inchoate, unschooled lovers, and yet rise to a
crescendo of romantic eloquence in the telling,
which is exactly what he does, and is why the
whole section is so deeply moving.

　　After *Nocturne* had made itself known to the

world at large, reactions to it were comically contradictory. Most of Swinnerton's associates praised it to the skies, in spite of his repeated insistence that the book was a mere nothing. Time and again, over a period of half a lifetime, he attempted to dismiss a work which he once confided had become something of an albatross round his neck. 'A literature composed of *Nocturnes* would be disastrous'; 'Those who have praised *Nocturne* very highly have been mistaken'; 'It has been extolled for the wrong reasons'. A few writers agreed with him, and it is typical of his perverse modesty that he should have taken such care to preserve in his autobiography the text of one of the most damning of all reactions to the book. In August 1918 Swinnerton received the following letter:

Dear Sir,

    I have read *Nocturne*. I must say you young writers (if you ARE young) spread your butter thin and make it go a long way. There are pages and pages of *Nocturne* that would not last me half a line.

    On the whole I found it a damned dismal book about people who ought not to exist. Don't you get tired of a world in which there is nothing but squalid poverty and women cut off about the waist? You impress me as a discouraged man discouraging other people. You may have your uses; but I wish you wouldn't.

    As to Wells, God forgive him! He has a kindly mania for praising people whom he ought to stir up by stupendous yawns in their faces. However, you make your people live all right enough. You would be much better employed in killing them. You also have a pathological nightmare in which, while striving towards a happy ending, you can never get it because a series of trivial and sordid obstacles continually interpose themselves. I get dreams like that when I am run down. Much of your pseudo-analysis of Jenny's processes is this and nothing else.

Don't you be petted and flattered by Rebecca (West) and H. G. W. You are only a wretched artist, with only one subject. But you are probably worth insulting. This is the object of this tonic letter. Look around a bit and let yourself rip.

Sincerely,
G. Bernard Shaw.

At the far end of the critical spectrum from this Shavian blast comes an anecdote which Swinnerton included in a later book of literary reminiscence:

Fitzgerald's *This Side of Paradise* was out, but I forget whether I heard of it. I met him once in London, when his reputation was that of a brash youngster approved by a highly troubled Galsworthy; and I hope not to be thought unkind if I record our brief encounter. I had recommended Chatto and Windus to publish *The Great Gatsby*. One day, just at lunch-time, I was told that Mr Fitzgerald wished to see the partners, but that both had already gone out: would

I see him? I went from my office to the waiting-room, where a young man sat, with his hat on, at a small table. He did not rise or remove his hat, and he did not answer my greeting, so I took another chair, expressing regret that no partner was available, and asked if there was anything I could do. Assuming, I suppose, that I was some base hireling, he continued brusque to the point of truculence; but we spoke of the purpose of his visit, and after a few moments he silently removed his hat. Two minutes later, looking rather puzzled, he rose. I did the same. I spoke warmly of *The Great Gatsby*; and his manner softened. He became an agreeable boy, quite ingenuous and inoffensive, and finally asked my name. I told him. If had said 'the Devil', he could not have been more horrified. Snatching up his hat in consternation, he cried, 'Oh, my God!. *Nocturne*'s one of my favourite books!', and dashed out of the premises. That was our only interview.

In retrospect, we may be excused for wondering how it came that two such shrewd judges of literary excellence should be so diametrically opposed in their views of what is, after all the least controversial of novels. Shaw, who had written five fictions of such startling originality that he could never find a publisher willing to take them on, clearly detested what Swinnerton had done; Fitzgerald, at the time of his encounter with Swinnerton one of the world's most widely acclaimed novelists, just as clearly was reduced to shambling idolatry the moment

he realised who Swinnerton was. It seems likely
that the very qualities which so outraged Shaw
about *Nocturne* were precisely those which so
vehemently engaged Fitzgerald's admiration.
What disgusted the Creative Evolutionist
enraptured the prose poet of unrequited love.
When Shaw says of Swinnerton's characters
that they were better dead, what he really
means is that they might just as well be dead
unless they dash out and join the Fabian
Society, from which fastness they can fight the
causes of their own miserable poverty with all
the ingenuity at their command. But the point
about people like Jenny and Em is that they
have no ingenuity. They are congenitally
quiescent in the face of circumstance, and are
informed by some blind instinct that to struggle
against the fate which has dumped them in
squalid rooms in Kennington Park,
surrounded them with the disspiriting odour of
eternal stew, and hedged them in with anxieties
about where the next penny is coming from,
would be impossibly grandiloquent of them.
Shaw is railing against a school of fiction which
he particularly detested, where the action is
carried forward, and the sympathies of the
reader engaged, through a succession of
introspective inner monologues, wherein the
leading character discloses her every random
thought. Faced with the mental processes of
Jenny as she weighs up her moral predicament,

Shaw would have polished off the whole
business in a few lines and pressed on to other
things, which is what he means in his letter
when he talks of the butter being spread thin,
and that there are 'pages and pages that would
not last me half a line'. On one occasion,
incensed by Bennett's fatuous claim that a
novel was harder to write than a play because
it was longer, Shaw had actually reduced the
piece-rate theory of literature to absurdity by
taking Macbeth's realization in Act V Scene 8
that his cause is doomed, and transmuting it
into a rambling inner monologue. Forty lines
of blank verse become more than two thousand
words of introspective maundering, couched
in 'the style of my friends Bennett and
Galsworthy when they are too lazy to write
plays'. And to those names Shaw might easily
have added Swinnerton's.

But Fitzgerald would have been moved to
admiration by the acute insight with which
Swinnerton portrays the contradictory emotions inspired by Jenny and Em each in the
other's breast. They hate each other. They love
each other. They envy each other. They
despise each other. They are jealous of each
other. They yearn for peace and contentment
for each other. And being the creatures they
are, they can never quite bring themselves to
express what their feelings are. And where did
Swinnerton acquire his perceptions regarding

the married state, laid out in the scene where Keith pleads on behalf of personal freedom and a casting off of the hated trammels of routine, to which Jenny responds by offering her idea of what wedded bliss always comes to in the end: 'I expect we shall tyrannize over each other. It seems to me that's what people do'? But then Jenny is almost as shrewd as her creator; in an early scene, when she sneers at the street fashions about her by likening her contemporaries to savages sporting bright beads, we are told that this is 'the constant amusement of the expert as she regards the amateur. She has all the satisfaction of knowing better, without the turmoil of competition, a fact which distinguishes the superior spirit from the struggling helot.'

Nocturne is something else too. It is essentially a London novel, in the sense that the brooding, minatory town is a major character in the story. From the grime of the back streets to the pristine gleam of the waters flowing swiftly under the bridge to the sea, from the rickety rooms in Kennington to the glamour of lighted shop windows, from the wearisome day to that magical moment when night falls and darkened streets begin to shine, it is London which seems to be holding the ring as the characters battle out their destiny. It is a town so hard and so vast as to be indifferent to the small comforts and reassurances of those who live within its boundaries. Of the girls' dead mother we are told:

She had been very much as Emmy now was, but a great deal more cheerful. She had been plump and fresh-coloured, and in spite of Pa Blanchard's ways she had led a happy life. In the old days there had been friends and neighbours, now all lost in course of removals from one part of London to another, so that the girls were without friends and knew intimately no women older than themselves.

As for the heroine of the story, she too has to take from the town what she can get; if it has shown her a hard face, she has learned from the experience:

Perhaps it was that she had too much pride—or that in general she saw life with too much self-complacency, or that she was not in the habit of yielding to disappointment. It may have been that Jenny belonged to that class of persons who are called self-sufficient. She plunged through a crisis with her own zest, meeting attack with counter-attack, keeping her head, surveying with the instinctive irreverence and self-protective wariness of the London urchin the possibilities and swaying fortunes of the fight.

Here at least we are in no doubt of the auto-biographical overtones of the writing; in one of his books of reminiscence, Swinnerton begins a sentence about himself with: 'Being a Londoner and incapable of reverence . . .'

The most interesting point of all about *Nocturne* is the degree to which its author was justified in dismissing it as a 'stunt' novel hardly worthy of all the attention it has received. Usually when a writer denies that he is thinking about what posterity will make of him, he is thinking of nothing else. But Swinnerton seems to have been perfectly sincere about his own indifference to his posthumous reputation. Time and again he predicts that within weeks of his death he and his work will be completely forgotten, and that he is content that this should be so. He adamantly refuses to agonize over his failure to be Dickens or Tolstoy: 'I was from the year 1902 writing novels. They were not good novels, because I am not a genius. But they were very short'. The temptation is to believe the man, for a very interesting reason. Of all the writers of his time, none was shrewder than Swinnerton in evaluating literary merit, marketplace viability, prospects of longevity. In his copies critical writings, disguised as discursive chapters of literary gossip, Swinnerton is like some great financier assessing the significance of the slightest shift in market values. Since the Great War this one has risen a few points, that one plummetted to obscurity; when fashions change so-and-so will enjoy from beyond the grave a popularity which would have surprised him, but his friend, whatshisname, will no longer be thought worth a glance. As a comprehensive form-book of the literary world as he knew it, his 'The Georgian Literary Scene' is worth a thousand academic tomes. Into that book he placed brief sketches of every considerable British writer of the century, accompanied by a summary of their published work and the possible reasons for its fortunes. Only one name is missing from this brilliantly entertaining cavalcade of ink and paper, that of Swinnerton himself. Was he being fair with himself in so ruthlessly excising himself from the literary annals? Was he correct in predicting that one day soon after his death people would not even remember his name, let alone his books? Let the reader now enjoy *Nocturne* and decide for himself.

Part One

EVENING

I. *SIX O'CLOCK*

SIX o'clock was striking. The darkness by
Westminster Bridge was intense; and as
the tramcar turned the corner from the
Embankment Jenny craned to look at the thickly
running water below. The glistening of reflected
lights which spotted the surface of the Thames
gave its rapid current an air of such mysterious
and especially sinister power that she was for an
instant aware of almost uncontrollable terror.
She could feel her heart beating, yet she could not
withdraw her gaze. It was nothing: no danger
threatened Jenny but the danger of uneventful
life; and her sense of sudden yielding to unknown
force was the merest fancy, to be quickly forgotten when the occasion had passed. None the
less, for that instant her dread was breathless. It
was the fear of one who walks in a wood, at an
inexplicable rustle. The darkness and the sense
of moving water continued to fascinate her, and
she slightly shuddered, not at a thought, but at
the sensation of the moment. At last she closed
her eyes, still, however, to see mirrored as in some
visual memory the picture she was trying to ignore.
In a faint panic, hardly conscious of her fear, she
stared at her neighbour's newspaper, spelling
out the headings to some of the paragraphs, until
the need of such protection was past.

As the car proceeded over the bridge, grinding its way through the still rolling echoes of the striking hour, it seemed part of an endless succession of such cars, all alike crowded with homeward-bound passengers, and all, to the curious mind, resembling ships that pass very slowly at night from safe harbourage to the unfathomable elements of the open sea. It was such a cold still night that the sliding windows of the car were almost closed, and the atmosphere of the covered upper deck was heavy with tobacco smoke. It was so dark that one could not see beyond the fringes of the lamplight upon the bridge. The moon was in its last quarter, and would not rise for several hours; and while the glitter of the city lay behind, and the sky was greyed with light from below, the surrounding blackness spread creeping fingers of night in every shadow.

The man sitting beside Jenny continued to puff steadfastly at his pipe, lost in the news, holding mechanically in his further hand the return ticket which would presently be snatched by the hurrying tram-conductor. He was a shabby middle-aged clerk with a thin beard, and so he had not the least interest for Jenny, whose eye was caught by other beauties than those of assiduous labour. She had not even to look at him to be quite sure that he did not matter to her. Almost, Jenny did not care whether he had glanced sideways at herself or not. She presently gave a quiet sigh of relief as at length the river

was left behind and the curious nervous tension
—no more lasting than she might have felt at
seeing a man balancing upon a high window-sill
—was relaxed. She breathed more deeply, perhaps, for a few instants; and then, quite naturally,
she looked at her reflection in the sliding glass.
That hat, as she could see in the first sure speedless survey, had got the droops. 'See about you!'
she said silently and threateningly, jerking her
head. The hat trembled at the motion, and was
thereafter ignored. Stealthily Jenny went back
to her own reflection in the window, catching
the clearly chiselled profile of her face, bereft in
the dark mirror of all its colour. She could see
her nose and chin quite white, and her lips as
part of the general colourless gloom. A little
white brooch at her neck stood boldly out; and
that was all that could be seen with any clear-
ness, as the light was not directly overhead. Her
eyes were quite lost, apparently, in deep shadows.
Yet she could not resist the delight of continuing
narrowly to examine herself. The face she saw
was hardly recognisable as her own; but it was
bewitchingly pale, a study in black and white,
the kind of face which, in a man, would at once
have drawn her attention and stimulated her
curiosity. She had longed to be pale, but the
pallor she was achieving by millinery work in a
stuffy room was not the marble whiteness which
she had desired. Only in the sliding window
could she see her face ideally transfigured. There

it had the brooding dimness of strange poetic romance. You couldn't know about that girl, she thought. You'd want to know about her. You'd wonder all the time about her, as though she had a secret. . . . The reflection became curiously distorted. Jenny was smiling to herself.

As soon as the tramcar had passed the bridge, lighted windows above the shops broke the magic mirror and gave Jenny a new interest, until, as they went onward, a shopping district, ablaze with colour, crowded with loitering people, and alive with din, turned all thoughts from herself into one absorbed contemplation of what was beneath her eyes. So absorbed was she, indeed, that the conductor had to prod her shoulder with his two fingers before he could recover her ticket and exchange it for another. ' 'Arf asleep, some people!' he grumbled, shoving aside the projecting arms and elbows which prevented his free passage between the seats. 'Feyuss please!' Jenny shrugged her shoulder, which seemed as though it had been irritated at the conductor's touch. It felt quite bruised. 'Silly old fool!' she thought, with a brusque glance. Then she went silently back to the contemplation of all the life that gathered upon the muddy and glistening pavements below.

II

In a few minutes they were past the shops and once again in darkness, grinding along, pitching

from end to end, the driver's bell clanging every
minute to warn carts and people off the tram-
lines. Once, with an awful thunderous grating
of the brakes, the car was pulled up, and everybody tried to see what had provoked the sense of
accident. There was a little shouting, and Jenny,
staring hard into the roadway, thought she could
see as its cause a small girl pushing a perambulator loaded with bundles of washing. Her first
impulse was pity—'Poor little thing'; but the
words were hardly in her mind before they were
chased away by a faint indignation at the child
for getting in the tram's way. Everybody ought
to look where they were going. Ev-ry bo-dy
ought to look where they were go-ing, said the
pitching tramcar. Ev-ry bo-dy . . . Oh, sickening! Jenny looked at her neighbour's paper—
her refuge. 'Striking speech,' she read. Whose?
What did it matter? Talk, talk . . . Why didn't
they do something? What were they to do?
The tram pitched to the refrain of a comic song:
'Actions speak louder than words!' That kid
who was wheeling the perambulator full of washing. . . . Jenny's attention drifted away like the
speech of one who yawns, and she looked again
at her reflection. The girl in the sliding glass
wouldn't say much. She'd think the more.
She'd say, when Sir Herbert pressed for his
answer, 'My thoughts are my own, Sir Herbert
Mainwaring.' What was it the girl in *One of the
Best* said? 'You may command an army of

soldiers; but you cannot still the beating of a woman's heart!' Silly fool, she was. Jenny had felt the tears in her eyes, burning, and her throat very dry, when the words had been spoken in the play; but Jenny at the theatre and Jenny here and now were different persons. Different? Why, there were fifty Jennys. But the shrewd, romantic, honest, true Jenny was behind them all, not stupid, not sentimental, bold as a lion, destructively experienced in hardship and endurance, very quick indeed to single out and wither humbug that was within her range of knowledge, but innocent as a child before any other sort of humbug whatsoever. That was why she could now sneer at the stage-heroine, and could play with the mysterious beauties of her own reflection; but it was why she could also be led into quick indignation by something read in a newspaper.

Tum-ty tum-ty tum-ty, said the tram. There were some more shops. There were straggling shops and full-blazing rows of shops. There were stalls along the side of the road, women dancing to an organ outside a public-house. Shops, shops, houses, houses, houses . . . light, darkness. . . . Jenny gathered her skirt. This was where she got down. One glance at the tragic lady of the mirror, one glance at the rising smoke that went to join the general cloud; and she was upon the iron-shod stairs of the car and into the greasy roadway. Then darkness, as she turned

along beside a big building into the side streets
among rows and rows of the small houses of
Kennington Park.

III

IT was painfully dark in these side streets. The
lamps threw beams such a short distance that
they were as useless as the hidden stars. Only
down each street one saw mild spots starting out
of the gloom, fascinating in their regularity, like
shining beads set at prepared intervals in a body
of jet. The houses were all in darkness, because
evening meals were laid in the kitchens: the
front rooms were all kept for Sunday use, excepting when the Emeralds and Edwins and Geralds
and Dorises were practising upon their mothers'
pianos. Then you could hear a din! But not
now. Now all was as quiet as night, and even
doors were not slammed. Jenny crossed the
street and turned a corner. On the corner itself
was a small chandler's shop, with 'Magnificent
Tea, per 2/- lb.'; 'Excellent Tea, per 1/8d. lb.';
'Good Tea, per 1/4d. lb.' advertised in great bills
upon its windows above a huge collection of unlikely goods gathered together like a happy
family in its tarnished abode. Jenny passed the
dully-lighted shop, and turned in at her own
gate. In a moment she was inside the house,
sniffing at the warm odour-laden air within
doors. Her mouth drew down at the corners.
Stew to-night! An amused gleam, lost upon the

dowdy passage, fled across her bright eyes.
Emmy wouldn't have thanked her for that!
Emmy—sick to death herself of the smell of
cooking—would have slammed down the pot in
despairing rage.

In the kitchen a table was laid; and Emmy
stretched her head back to peer from the scullery,
where she was busy at the gas stove. She did not
say a word. Jenny also was speechless; and went
as if without thinking to the kitchen cupboard.
The table was only half-laid as usual; but that
fact did not make her action the more palatable
to Emmy. Emmy, who was older than Jenny by
a mysterious period—diminished by herself, but
kept at its normal term of three years by Jenny,
except in moments of some heat, when it grew
for purposes of retort,—was also less effective in
many ways, such as in appearance and in adroitness; and Jenny comprised in herself, as it were,
the good looks of the family. Emmy was the
housekeeper, who looked after Pa Blanchard;
Jenny was the roving blade who augmented Pa's
pension by her own fluctuating wages. That was
another slight barrier between the sisters. Nevertheless, Emmy was quite generous enough, and
was long-suffering, so that her resentment took
the general form of silences and secret broodings
upon their different fortunes. There was a great
deal to be said about this difference, and the
saying grew more and more remote from explicit
utterance as thought of it ground into Emmy's

mind through long hours and days and weeks of solitude. Pa could not hear anything besides the banging of pots, and he was too used to sudden noises to take any notice of such a thing; but the pots themselves, occasionally dented in savage dashes against each other or against the taps, might have heard vicious apostrophes if they had listened intently to Emmy's ejaculations. As it was, with the endurance of pots, they mutely bore their scars and waited dumbly for super-annuation. And every bruise stood to Emmy when she renewed acquaintance with it as mark of yet another grievance against Jenny. For Jenny enjoyed the liberties of this life while Emmy stayed at home. Jenny sported, while Emmy was engaged upon the hideous routine of kitchen affairs, and upon the nursing of a com-paratively helpless old man who could do hardly anything at all for himself.

Pa was in his bedroom,—the back room on the ground-floor, chosen because he could not walk up the stairs, but must have as little trouble in self-conveyance as possible,—staggeringly making his toilet for the meal to come, sitting patiently in front of his dressing-table by the light of a solitary candle. He would appear in due course, when he was fetched. He had been a strong man, a runner and cricketer in his youth, and rather obstreperously disposed; but that time was past, and his strength for such pur-suits was as dead as the wife who had suffered because of its vagaries. He could no longer disappear on the Saturdays, as he had been used to do in the old days. His chair in the kitchen, the horse-hair sofa in the sitting-room, the bed in the bedroom, were the only changes he now had from one day's end to another. Emmy and Jenny, pledges of a real but not very delicate affection, were all that remained to call up the sorrowful thoughts of his old love, and those old times of virility, when Pa and his strength and his rough boisterousness had been the delight of perhaps a dozen regular companions. He sometimes looked at the two girls with a passionless scrutiny, as though he were trying to remember something buried in ancient neglect; and his eyes would thereafter, perhaps at the mere sense of helplessness, fill slowly with tears, until Emmy, smothering her own rough sympathy, would dab Pa's eyes with a harsh handkerchief and would rebuke him for his decay. Those were hard moments in the Blanchard home, for the two girls had grown almost manlike in abhorrence of tears, and with this masculine distaste had arisen a corresponding feeling of powerlessness in face of emotion which they could not share. It was as though Pa had become something like an old and beloved dog, unable to speak, pitied and despised, yet claiming by his very dumbness something that they could only give by means of pats and half-bullying kindness. At such times it was Jenny who left her place at the table and popped a morsel of food into Pa's mouth; but it was Emmy who best understood the bitterness of his soul. It was Emmy, therefore, who would snap at her sister and bid her get on with her own food; while Pa Blanchard made trembling scrapes with his knife and fork until the mood passed. But then it was Emmy who was most with Pa; it was Emmy who hated him in the middle of her love because he stood to her as the living symbol of her daily inescapable servitude in this household. Jenny could never have felt that she would like to kill Pa. Emmy sometimes felt that. She at times, when he had been provoking or obtuse, so shook with hysterical anger, born of the inevitable days in his society and in the kitchen, that she could have thrown at him the battered pot which she carried, or could have pushed him passionately against the mantelpiece in her fierce hatred of his helplessness and his occasional perverse stupidity. He was rarely stupid with Jenny, but giggled at her teasing.

Jenny was taller than Emmy by several inches. She was tall and thin and dark, with an air of something like impudent bravado that made her expression sometimes a little wicked. Her nose was long and straight, almost sharp-pointed; her face too thin to be a perfect oval. Her eyes were wide open, and so full of power to show feeling that they seemed constantly alive with changing and mocking lights and shadows. If she had been stouter the excellent shape of her body, now almost too thick at the waist, would have been emphasised. Happiness and comfort, a decrease in physical as in mental restlessness, would have made her more than ordinarily beautiful. As it was she drew the eye at once, as though she challenged a conflict of will; and her movements were so swift and eager, so little clumsy or jerking, that Jenny had a carriage to command admiration. The resemblance between the sisters was ordinarily not noticeable. It would have needed a photograph—because photographs, besides flattening the features, also in some manner 'compose' and distinguish them—to reveal the likenesses in shape, in shadow, even in outline, which were momentarily obscured by the natural differences of colouring and expression. Emmy was less dark, more temperamentally unadventurous, stouter, and possessed of more colour. She was twenty-eight or possibly twenty-nine, and her mouth was rather too hard for pleasantness. It was not peevish, but the lips were set as though she had endured much. Her eyes, also, were hard; although if she cried one saw her face soften remarkably into the semblance of that of a little girl. From an involuntary defiance her expression changed to something really pathetic. One could not help loving her then, not with the free give and take of happy affection, but with a shamed hope that nobody could read the conflict of sympathy and contempt which made one's love frigid and self-conscious. Jenny rarely cried:

her cheeks reddened and her eyes grew full of tears; but she did not cry. Her tongue was too ready and her brain too quick for that. Also, she kept her temper from flooding over into the self-abandonment of angry weeping and vitupera-tion. Perhaps it was that she had too much pride—or that in general she saw life with too much self-complacency, or that she was not in the habit of yielding to disappointment. It may have been that Jenny belonged to that class of persons who are called self-sufficient. She plunged through a crisis with her own zest, meeting attack with counter-attack, keeping her head, surveying with the instinctive irreverence and self-protective wariness of the London urchin the possibilities and swaying fortunes of the fight. Emmy, so much slower, so much less self-reliant, had no refuge but in scolding that grew shriller and more shrill until it ended in violent weeping, a withdrawal from the field entirely abject. She was not a born fighter. She was harder on the surface, but weaker in powers below the surface. Her long solitudes had made her build up griev-ances, and devastating thoughts, had given her a thousand bitter things to fling into the conflict; but they had not strengthened her character, and she could not stand the strain of prolonged argument. Sooner or later she would abandon everything, exhausted, and beaten into impo-tence. She could bear more, endure more, than Jenny; she could bear much, so that the story of her life might be read as one long scene of endurance of things which Jenny would have struggled madly to overcome or to escape. But having borne for so long, she could fight only like a cat, her head as it were turned aside, her fur upon end, stealthily moving paw by paw, always keeping her front to the foe but seeking for escape—until the pride perilously supporting her temper gave way and she dissolved into incoherence and quivering sobs.

It might have been said roughly that Jenny more closely resembled her father, whose temperament in her care-free happy-go-lucky way she understood very well (better than Emmy did), and that while she carried into her affairs a necessarily more delicate refinement than his she had still the dare-devil spirit that Pa's friends had so much admired. She had more humour than Emmy—more power to laugh, to be detached, to be indifferent. Emmy had no such power. She could laugh; but she could only laugh seriously, or at obviously funny things. Otherwise, she felt everything too much. As Jenny would have said, she 'couldn't take a joke.' It made her angry, or puzzled, to be laughed at. Jenny laughed back, and tried to score a point in return, not always scrupulously. Emmy put a check on her tongue. She was sometimes virtuously silent. Jenny rarely put a check on her tongue. She sometimes let it say perfectly outrageous things, and was surprised at the consequences. For her it was enough that she had not meant to hurt. She sometimes hurt very much. She frequently hurt Emmy to the quick, darting in one of her sure careless stabs that shattered Emmy's self-control. So while they loved each other, Jenny also despised Emmy, while Emmy in return hated and was jealous of Jenny, even to the point of actively wishing in moments of furtive and shame-faced savageness to harm her. That was the outward difference between the sisters in time of stress. Of their inner, truer selves it would be more rash to speak, for in times of peace Jenny had innumerable insights and emotions that would be forever unknown to the older girl. The sense of rivalry, however, was acute: it coloured every moment of their domestic life, unwinking and incessant. When Emmy came from the scullery into the kitchen bearing her precious dish of stew, and when Jenny, standing up, was measured against her, this rivalry could have been seen by any skilled observer. It rayed and forked about them as lightning might have done about two adjacent trees. Emmy put down her dish.

'Fetch Pa, will you!' she said briefly. One could see who gave orders in the kitchen.

IV

JENNY found her father in his bedroom, sitting before the dressing-table upon which a tall candle stood in an equally tall candlestick. He was looking intently at his reflection in the looking-glass, as one who encounters and examines a stranger. In the glass his face looked red and ugly, and the tossed grey hair and heavy beard were made to appear startlingly unkempt. His mouth was open, and his eyes shaded by lowered lids. In a rather trembling voice he addressed Jenny upon her entrance.

'Is supper ready?' he asked. 'I heard you come in.'

'Yes, Pa,' said Jenny. 'Aren't you going to brush your hair? Got a fancy for it like that, have you? My! What a man! With his shirt unbuttoned and his tie out. Come here! Let's have a look at you!' Although her words were unkind her tone was not, and as she rectified his omissions and put her arm round him Jenny gave her father a light tug. 'All right, are you? Been a good boy?'

'Yes . . . a good boy . . .' he feebly and waveringly responded. 'What's the noos to-night, Jenny?'

Jenny considered. It made her frown, so concentrated was her effort to remember.

'Well, somebody's made a speech,' she volunteered. 'They can all do that, can't they! And somebody's paid five hundred pounds transfer for Jack Sutherdon . . . is it Barnsley or Burnley? . . . And—oh, a fire at Southwark. . . . Just the usual sort of news, Pa. No murders. . . .'

'Ah, they don't have the murders they used to have,' grumbled the old man.

'That's the police, Pa.' Jenny wanted to re-assure him.

'I don't know how it is,' he trembled, stiffening his body and rising from the chair.

'Perhaps they hush 'em up?' That was a shock to him. He could not move until the notion had sunk into his head. 'Or perhaps people are more careful. . . . Don't get leaving themselves about like they used to.'

Pa Blanchard had no suggestion. Such perilous ideas, so frequently started by Jenny for his mystification, joggled together in his brain and made there the subject of a thousand ruminations. They tantalised Pa's slowly revolving thoughts, and kept these moving through long hours of silence. Such notions preserved his interest in the world, and his senile belief in Magic, as nothing else could have done.

Together, their pace suited to his step, the two moved slowly to the door. It took a long time to make the short journey, though Jenny supported her father on the one side and he used a stick in his right hand. In the passage he waited while she blew out his candle; and then they went forward to the meal. At the approach Pa's eyes opened wider, and luminously glowed.

'Is there dumplings?' he quivered, seeming to tremble with excitement.

'One for you, Pa!' cried Emmy from the kitchen. Pa gave a small chuckle of joy. His progress was accelerated. They reached the table, and

Emmy took his right arm for the descent into a substantial chair. Upon Pa's plate glistened a fair dumpling, a glorious mountain of paste amid the wreckage of meat and gravy. 'And now, perhaps,' Emmy went on, smoothing back from her forehead a little streamer of hair, 'you'll close the door, Jenny. . . .'

It was closed with a bang that made Pa jump and Emmy look savagely up.

'Sorry!' cried Jenny. 'How's that dumpling, Pa?' She sat recklessly at the table.

v

To look at the three of them sitting there munching away was a sight not altogether pleasing. Pa's veins stood out from his forehead, and the two girls devoted themselves to the food as if they needed it. There was none of the airy talk that goes on in the houses of the rich while maids or menservants come respectfully to right or left of the diners with decanters or dishes. Here the food was the thing, and there was no speech. Sometimes Pa's eyes rolled, sometimes Emmy glanced up with unconscious malevolence at Jenny, sometimes Jenny almost winked at the lithograph portrait of Edward the Seventh (as Prince of Wales) which hung over the mantelpiece above the one-and-tenpenny-ha'penny clock that ticked away so busily there. Something had happened long ago to Edward the Seventh, and he had a stain across his Field

Marshal's uniform. Something had happened also to the clock, which lay upon its side, as if kicking in a death agony. Something had happened to almost everything in the kitchen. Even the plates on the dresser, and the cups and saucers that hung or stood upon the shelves, bore the noble scars of service. Every time Emmy turned her glance upon a damaged plate, as sharp as a stalactite, she had the thought: 'Jenny's doing.' Every time she looked at the convulsive clock Emmy said to herself: 'That was Miss Jenny's cleverness when she chucked the cosy at Alf.' And when Emmy said in this reflective silence of animosity the name 'Alf' she drew a deep breath and looked straight up at Jenny with inscrutable eyes of pain.

VI

THE stew being finished, Emmy collected the plates, and retired once again to the scullery. Now did Jenny show afresh that curiosity whose first flush had been so ill-satisfied by the meat course. When, however, Emmy reappeared with that most domestic of sweets a bread pudding, Jenny's face fell once more; for of all dishes she most abominated bread pudding. Under her breath she adversely commented.

'Oh lor!' she whispered. 'Stew and b. p. What a life!'

Emmy, not hearing, but second sighted on such matters, shot a malevolent glance from her place. In an awful voice, intended to be a trifle arch, she addressed her father.

'Bready butter pudding, Pa?' she inquired. The old man whinnied with delight, and Emmy was appeased. She had one satisfied client, at any rate. She cut into the pudding with a knife, producing wedges with a dexterous hand.

'Hey ho!' observed Jenny to herself, tastelessly beginning the work of laborious demolition.

'Jenny thinks it's common. She ought to have the job of getting the meals!' cried Emmy, bitterly, obliquely attacking her sister by talking at her. 'Something to talk about then!' she sneered with chagrin, up in arms at a criticism.

'Well, the truth is,' drawled Jenny . . . 'If you want it . . . I don't like bread pudding.' Somehow she had never said that before, in all the years; but it seemed to her that bread pudding was like ashes in the mouth. It was like duty, or funerals, or . . . stew.

'The stuff's *got* to be finished up!' flared Emmy defiantly, with a sense of being adjudged inferior because she had dutifully habituated herself to the appreciation of bread pudding. 'You might think of that! What else am I to do?'

'That's just it, old girl. Just why I don't like it. I just *hate* to feel I'm finishing it up. Same with stew. I know it's been something else first. It's not *fresh*. Same old thing, week in, week out. Finishing up the scraps!'

'Proud stomach!' A quick flush came into Emmy's cheeks; and tears started to her eyes.

'Perhaps it is. Oh, but Em! Don't you feel like that yourself. . . . Sometimes? O-o-h! . . .' She drawled the word wearily. 'Oh for a bit more money! Then we could give stew to the cat's-meat man and bread to old Thompson's chickens. And then we could have nice things to eat. Nice birds and pastry . . . and trifle, and ices, and wine. . . . Not all this muck!'

'Muck!' cried Emmy, her lips seeming to thicken. 'When I'm so hot . . . And sick of it all! *You* go out; you do just exactly what you like. . . . And then you come home and. . . .' She began to gulp. 'What about me?'

'Well, it's just as bad for both of us!' Jenny did not think so really; but she said it. She thought Emmy had the bread and butter pudding nature, and that she did not greatly care what she ate so long as it was not too fattening. Jenny thought of Emmy as born for housework and cooking—of stew and bread puddings. For herself she had dreamed a nobler destiny, a destiny of romance, of delicious unknown things, romantic and indescribably exciting. She was to have the adventures, because she needed them. Emmy didn't need them. It was all very well for Emmy to say 'What about me?' It was no business of hers what happened to Emmy. They were different. Still, she repeated more confidently because there had been no immediate retort:

'Well, it's just as bad for both of us! *Just* as bad!'

' 'Tisn't! You're out all day—doing what you like!'

'Oh!' Jenny's eyes opened with theatrical wideness at such a perversion of the facts. 'Doing what I like! The millinery!'

'You are! You don't have to do all the scraping to make things go round, like I have to. No, you don't! Here have I . . . been in this . . . place slaving! Hour after hour! I wish *you'd* try and manage better. I bet you'd be thankful to finish up the scraps some way—any old way! I'd like to see *you* do what I do!'

Momentarily Jenny's picture of Emmy's nature (drawn accommodatingly by herself in order that her own might be differentiated and exalted by any comparison) was shattered. Emmy's vehemence had thus the temporary effect of creating a fresh reality out of a common idealisation of circumstance. The legend would re-form later, perhaps, and would continue so to re-form as persuasion flowed back upon Jenny's egotism, until it crystallised hard and became unchallengeable; but at any rate for this instant Jenny had had a glimmer of insight into that tamer discontent and rebelliousness that encroached like a canker upon Emmy's originally sweet nature. The shock of impact with unpleasant conviction made Jenny hasten to dissemble her real belief in Emmy's born inferiority. Her note was changed from one of complaint into one of persuasive entreaty.

'It's not that. It's not that. Not at all. But wouldn't you like a change from stew and bread pudding yourself? Sometimes, I mean. You *seem* to like it all right.' At that ill-considered suggestion, made with unintentional savageness, Jenny so worked upon herself that her own colour rose high. Her temper became suddenly unmanageable. 'You talk about me being out!' she breathlessly exclaimed. 'When do I go out? When! Tell me!'

'O-o-h! I *like* that! What about going to the pictures with Alf Rylett?' Emmy's hands were jerking upon the table in her anger. 'You're always out with him.'

'Me? Well I never! I'm not. When——'

They were interrupted unexpectedly by a feeble and jubilant voice.

'More bready butter pudding!' said Pa Blanchard, tipping his plate to show that he had finished.

'Yes, Pa!' For the moment Emmy was distracted from her feud. In a mechanical way, as mothers sometimes, deep in conversation, attend to their children's needs, she put another wedge of pudding upon the plate. 'Well, I say you *are*,' she resumed in the same strained voice. 'And tell me when *I* go out! I go out shopping. That's all. But for that, I'm in the house day and night. You don't care tuppence about Alf

—you wouldn't, not if he was walking the soles
off his boots to come to you. You never think
about him. He's like dirt, to you. Yet you go
out with him time after time. . . .' Her lips as
she broke off were pursed into a trembling unhappy pout, sure forerunner of tears. Her voice
was weak with feeling. The memory of lonely
evenings surged into her mind, evenings when
Jenny was out with Alf, while she, the drudge,
stayed at home with Pa, until she was desperate
with the sense of unutterable wrong. 'Time after
time, you go.'

'Sorry, I'm sure!' flung back Jenny, fairly in
the fray, too quick to read the plain message of
Emmy's tone and expression, too cruel to re-
linquish the sudden advantage. 'I never guessed
you wanted him. I wouldn't have done it for
worlds. You never *said*, you know!' Satirically,
she concluded, with a studiously careful accent,
which she used when she wanted to indicate
scorn or innuendo, 'I'm sorry. I ought to have
asked if I might!' Then, with a dash into grim-
mer satire: 'Why doesn't he ask you to go with
him? Funny his asking me, isn't it?'

Emmy grew violently crimson. Her voice had
a roughness in it. She was mortally wounded.

'Anybody'd know you were a lady!' she said
warmly.

'They're welcome!' retorted Jenny. Her eyes
flashed, glittering in the paltry gaslight. 'He's
never . . . Emmy, I didn't know you were such a

silly little fool. Fancy going on like that . . .
about a man like him. At your age!'

Vehement glances flashed between them. All
Emmy's jealousy was in her face, clear as day.
Jenny drew a sharp breath. Then, obstinately,
she closed her lips, looking for a moment like the
girl in the sliding window, inscrutable. Emmy,
also recovering herself, spoke again, trying to
steady her voice.

'It's not what you think. But I can't bear to
see you . . . playing about with him. It's not fair.
He thinks you mean it. You don't!'

'Course I don't. I don't mean anything. A
fellow like that!' Jenny laughed a little, wound-
ingly.

'What's the matter with him?' Savagely
Emmy betrayed herself again. She was trembling
from head to foot, her mind blundering hither
and thither for help against a quicker-witted foe.
'It's only *you* he's not good enough for,' she said
passionately. 'What's the matter with him?'

Jenny considered, her pale face now deadly
white, all the heat gone from her cheeks, though
the hard glitter remained in her eyes, cruelly
indicating the hunger within her bosom.

'Oh, he's all right in his way,' she drawlingly
admitted. 'He's clean. That's in his favour.
But he's quiet . . . he's got no devil in him. Sort
of man who tells you what he likes for breakfast.
I only go with him . . . well, you know why, as
well as I do. He's all right enough, as far as he

goes. But he's never on for a bit of fun. That's
it: he's got no devil in him. I don't like that
kind. Prefer the other sort.'

During this speech Emmy had kept back bitter
interruptions by an unparalleled effort. It had
seemed as though her fury had flickered, blazing
and dying away as thought and feeling struggled
together for mastery. At the end of it, however,
and at Jenny's declared preference for men of
devil, Emmy's face hardened.

'You be careful, my girl,' she prophesied with
a warning glance of anger. 'If that's the kind
you're after. Take care you're not left!'

'Oh, I can take care,' Jenny said, with cold
nonchalance. 'Trust me!'

VII

LATER, when they were both in the chilly scullery,
washing up the supper dishes, they were again
constrained. Somehow when they were alone
together they could not quarrel: it needed the
presence of Pa Blanchard to stimulate them to
retort. In his rambling silences they found the
spur for their unkind eloquence, and too often
Pa was used as a stalking-horse for their angers.
He could hardly hear, and could not follow the
talk; but by directing a remark to him, so that it
cannoned off at the other, each obtained satisfaction for the rivalry that endured from day to
day between them. Their hungry hearts, all the
latent bitternesses in their natures, yearning for

expression, found it in his presence. But alone, whatever their angers, they were generally silent. It may have been that their love was strong, or that their courage failed, or that the energy required for conflict was not aroused. That they deeply loved one another was sure; there was rivalry, jealousy, irritation between them, but it did not affect their love. The jealousy was a part of their general discontent—a jealousy that would grow more intense as each remained frustrate and unhappy. Neither understood the forces at work within herself; each saw these perversely illustrated in the other's faults. In each case the cause of unhappiness was unsatisfied love, unsatisfied craving for love. It was more acute in Emmy's case, because she was older and because the love she needed was under her eyes being wasted upon Jenny—if it were love, and not that mixture of admiration and desire with self-esteem that goes to make the common formula to which the name of love is generally attached. Jenny could not be jealous of Emmy as Emmy was jealous of Jenny. She had no cause; Emmy was not her rival. Jenny's rival was life itself, as will be shown hereafter: she had her own pain.

It was thus only natural that the two girls, having pushed Pa's chair to the side of the kitchen fire, and having loaded and set light to Pa's pipe, should work together in silence for a few minutes, clearing the table and washing the supper dishes. They were distant, both aggrieved; Emmy with

labouring breath and a sense of bitter animosity,
Jenny with the curled lip of one triumphant who
does not need her triumph and would abandon
it at the first move of forgiveness. They could
not speak. The work was done, and Emmy was
rinsing the washing basin, before Jenny could
bring herself to say awkwardly what she had in
her mind.

'Em,' she began. 'I didn't know you . . . you
know.' A silence. Emmy continued to swirl the
water round with the small washing-mop, her
face averted. Jenny's lip stiffened. She made
another attempt, to be the last, restraining her
irritation with a great effort. 'If you like I won't
. . . I won't go out with him any more.'

'Oh, you needn't worry,' Emmy doggedly said,
with her teeth almost clenched. 'I'm not worry-
ing about it.' She tried then to keep silent; but
the words were forced from her wounded heart.
With uncontrollable sarcasm she said: 'It's very
good of you, I'm sure!'

'Em!' It was coaxing. Jenny went nearer.
Still there was no reply. 'Em . . . don't be a silly
cat. If he'd only ask *you* to go once or twice, he'd
always want to. You needn't worry about me
being . . . See, I like somebody else—another
fellow. He's on a ship. Nowhere near here. I
only go with Alf because . . . Well, after all, he's
a man; and they're scarce. Suppose I leave off
going with him. . . .'

Both knew she had nothing but kind intention,

as in fact the betrayal of her own secret proved; but as Jenny could not keep out of her voice the slightest tinge of complacent pity, so Emmy could not accept anything so intolerable as pity.

'Thanks,' she said in perfunctory refusal; 'but you can do what you like. Just what you like.' She was implacable. She was drying the basin, her face hidden. 'I'm not going to take your leavings.' At that her voice quivered and had again that thread of roughness in it which had been there earlier. 'Not likely!'

'Well, I can't help it, can I!' cried Jenny, out of patience. 'If he likes me best. If he *won't* come to you. I mean, if I say I won't go out with him —will that put him on to you or send him off altogether? Em, do be sensible. Really, I never knew. Never dreamt of it. I've never wanted him. It's not as though he'd whistled and I'd gone trotting after him. Em! You get so ratty about——'

'Superior!' cried Emmy, gaspingly. 'Look down on me!' She was for an instant hysterical, speaking loudly and weepingly. Then she was close against Jenny; and they were holding each other tightly, while Emmy's dreadful quiet sobs shook both of them to the heart. And Jenny, above her sister's shoulder, could see through the window the darkness that lay without; and her eyes grew tender at an unbidden thought, which made her try to force herself to see through the darkness, as though she were sending a speechless

message to the unknown. Then, feeling Emmy
still sobbing in her arms, she looked down, laying
her face against her sister's face. A little contemptuous smile appeared in her eyes, and her
brow furrowed. Well, Emmy could cry. *She*
couldn't. She didn't want to cry. She wanted
to go out in the darkness that so pleasantly en-
wrapped the earth, back to the stir and glitter of
life somewhere beyond. Abruptly Jenny sighed.
Her vision had been far different from this scene.
It had carried her over land and sea right into an
unexplored realm where there was wild laughter
and noise, where hearts broke tragically and
women in the hour of ruin turned triumphant
eyes to the glory of life, and where blinding
streaming lights and scintillating colours made
everything seem different, made it seem romantic, rapturous, indescribable. From that vision
back to the cupboard-like house in Kennington
Park, and stodgy Alf Rylett, and supper of stew
and bread and butter pudding, and Pa, and this
little sobbing figure in her arms, was an incon-
gruous flight. It made Jenny's mouth twist in a
smile so painful that it was almost a grimace.

'Oh lor!' she said again, under her breath, as
she had said it earlier. '*What* a life!'

II. *THE TREAT*

I

GRADUALLY Emmy's tearless sobs diminished; she began to murmur broken meaningless ejaculations of self-contempt; and to strain away from Jenny. At last she pushed Jenny from her, feverishly freeing herself, so that they stood apart, while Emmy blew her nose and wiped her eyes. All this time they did not speak to each other, and when Emmy turned blindly away Jenny mechanically took hold of the kettle, filled it, and set it to boil upon the gas. Emmy watched her curiously, feeling that her nose was cold and her eyes were burning. Little dry tremors seemed to shake her throat; dreariness had settled upon her, pressing her down, making her feel ashamed of such a display of the long secret so carefully hoarded away from prying glances.

'What's that for?' she miserably asked, indicating the kettle.

'Going to steam my hat,' Jenny said. 'The brim's all floppy.' There was now only a practical note in her voice. She too was ashamed. 'You'd better go up and lie down for a bit. I'll stay with Pa, in case he falls into the fire. Just the sort of thing he *would* do on a night like this. Just because you're upset.'

'I shan't go up. It's too cold. I'll sit by the fire a bit.'

460

They both went into the kitchen, where the old man was whistling under his breath.

'Was there any noos on the play-cards?' he inquired after a moment, becoming aware of their presence. 'Emmy—Jenny.'

'No, Pa. I told you. Have to wait till Sunday. Funny thing there's so much more news in the Sunday papers. I suppose people are all extra wicked on Saturdays. They get paid Friday night, I shouldn't wonder; and it goes to their heads.'

'Silly!' Emmy said under her breath. 'It's the week's news.'

'That's all right, old girl,' admonished Jenny. 'I was only giving him something to think about. Poor old soul. Now, about this hat: the girls all go on at me. . . . Say I dress like a broker's-man. I'm going to smarten myself up. You never know what might happen. Why, I might get off with a Duke!'

Emmy was overtaken by an impulse of gratitude.

'You can have mine, if you like,' she said. 'The one you gave me . . . on my birthday.' Jenny solemnly shook her head. She did not thank her sister. Thanks were never given in that household, because they were a part of 'peliteness,' and were supposed to have no place in the domestic arena.

'Not if I know it!' she humorously retorted. 'I made it for you, and it suits you. Not my style at all. I'll just get out my box of bits. You'll see something that'll surprise you, my girl.'

The box proved to contain a large number of 'bits' of all sizes and kinds—fragments of silk (plain and ribbed), of plush, of ribbon both wide and narrow; small sprays of marguerites, a rose or two, some poppies, and a bunch of violets; a few made bows in velvet and silk; some elastic, some satin, some feathers, a wing here and there . . . the miscellaneous assortment of odds-and-ends always appropriated (or, in the modern military slang, 'won') by assistants in the millinery. Some had been used, some were startlingly new. Jenny was more modest in such acquirements than were most of her associates; but she was affected, as all such must be, by the prevailing wind. Strangely enough, it was not her habit to wear very smart hats, for business, or at any other time. She would have told you, in the event of any such remark, that when you had been fiddling about with hats all day you had other things to do in the evenings. Yet she had good taste and very nimble fingers when occasion arose. In bringing her box from the bedroom she brought also from the stand in the passage her drooping hat, against which she proceeded to lay various materials, trying them with her sure eye, seeking to compose a picture, with that instinctive sense of cynosure which marks the crafty expert. Fascinated, with her lips parted in an expression of that stupidity which

is so often the sequel to a fit of crying, Emmy
watched Jenny's proceedings, her eyes travelling
from the hat to the ever-growing heap of dis-
carded ornaments. She was dully impressed
with the swift judgment of her sister in consulting
the secrets of her inner taste. It was a judgment
unlike anything in her own nature of which she
was aware, excepting the measurement of ingredients for a pudding.

So they sat, all engrossed, while the kettle
began to sing, and the desired steam to pour
from the spout, clouding the scullery. The only
sound that arose was the gurgling of Pa Blanchard's pipe (for he was what is called in Kennington Park a wet smoker). He sat remembering
something or pondering the insufficiency of news.
Nobody ever knew what he thought about in his
silences. It was a mystery over which the girls
did not puzzle because they were themselves in
the habit of sitting for long periods without
speech. Pa's broodings were as customary to
them as the absorbed contemplativeness of a
baby. 'Give him his pipe,' as Jenny said; 'and
he'll be quiet for hours—till it goes out. *Then*
there's a fuss! My word, what a racket! Talk
about a fire alarm!' And on such occasions she
would mimic him ridiculingly, to diminish his
complaints, while Emmy roughly relighted the
hubble-bubble and patted her father once more
into a contented silence. Pa was to them, although they did not know it, their bond of union.

Without him, they would have fallen apart, like the outer pieces of a wooden boot-tree. For his sake, with all the apparent lack of sympathy shown in their behaviour to him, they endured a life which neither desired or would have tolerated upon her own account. So it was that Pa's presence acted as a check and served them as company of a meagre kind, although he was less interesting or expansive than a little dog might have been.

When Jenny went out to the scullery carrying her hat, after sweeping the scraps she had declined back into the old draper's cardboard box which amply contained such treasures and preserved them from dust, Emmy, now quite quiet again, continued to sit by the fire, staring at the small glowing strip that showed under the door of the kitchen grate. Every now and then she would sigh, wearily closing her eyes; and her breast would rise as if with a sob. And she would sometimes look slowly up at the clock, with her head upon one side in order to see the hands in their proper aspect, as if she were calculating.

II

FROM the scullery came the sound of Jenny's whistle as she cheerily held the hat over the steam. Pa heard it as something far away, like a distant salvationists' band, and pricked up his ears; Emmy heard it, and her brow was

contracted. Her expression darkened. Jenny
began to hum:

' "*Oh Liza, sweet Liza,*
  If you die an old maid, you'll have only yourself to
      blame. . . ."'

It was like a sudden noise in a forest at night,
so poignant was the contrast of the radiating
silences that succeeded. Jenny's voice stopped
sharply. Perhaps it had occurred to her that her
song would be overheard. Perhaps she had herself become affected by the meaning of the words
she was so carelessly singing. There was once
more an air of oblivion over all things. The old
man sank back in his chair, puffing slowly, blue
smoke from the bowl of the pipe, grey smoke
from between his lips. Emmy looked again at
the clock. She had the listening air of one who
awaits a bewildering event. Once she shivered,
and bent to the fire, raking among the red tum-
bling small coal with the bent kitchen poker.
Jenny began to whistle again, and Emmy impatiently wriggled her shoulders, jarred by the
noise. Suddenly she could bear no longer the
whistle that pierced her thoughts and distracted
her attention, but went out to the scullery.

'How are you getting on?' she asked with an
effort.

'Fine. This gas leaks. Can't you whiff it?
Don't know which one it is. Pa all right?'

'Yes, he's all right. Nearly finished?'

'Getting on. Tram nearly ran over a kid to-night. She was wheeling a pram full of washing on the line. There wasn't half a row about it—shouting and swearing. Anybody would have thought the kid had laid down on the line. I expect she was frightened out of her wits—all those men shouting at her. There, now I'll lay it on the plate rack over the gas for a bit. . . . Look smart, shan't I! With a red rose in it and a red ribbon. . . .'

'Not going to have those streamers, or any lace, are you?'

'Not likely. You see the kids around here wearing them; but the kids round here are always a season late. Same with their costumes. They don't know any better. I do!'

Jenny was cheerfully contemptuous. She knew what was being worn along Regent Street and in Bond Street, because she saw it with her own eyes. Then she came home and saw the girls of her own district swanking about like last year's patterns, as she said. She couldn't help laughing at them. It made her think of the tales of savages wearing top hats with strings of beads and thinking they were all in the latest European fashion. That is the constant amusement of the expert as she regards the amateur. She has all the satisfaction of knowing better, without the turmoil of competition, a fact which distinguishes the superior spirit from the struggling helot. Jenny took full advantage of her situation and her knowledge.

'Yes, you know a lot,' Emmy said dryly.

'Ah, you've noticed it?' Jenny was not to be gibed at without retort. 'I'm glad.'

'So *you* think,' Emmy added, as though she had not heard the reply.

There came at this moment a knock at the front door. Emmy swayed, grew pale, and then slowly reddened until the colour spread to the very edges of her bodice. The two girls looked at one another, a deliberate interchange of glances that was at the same time, upon both sides, an intense scrutiny. Emmy was breathing heavily; Jenny's nostrils were pinched.

'Well,' at last said Jenny, drawlingly. 'Didn't you hear the knock? Aren't you going to answer it?' She reached as she spoke to the hat lying upon the plate rack above the gas stove, looking fixedly away from her sister. Her air of gravity was unchanged. Emmy, hesitating, made as if to speak, to implore something; but, being repelled, she turned, and went thoughtfully across the kitchen to the front door. Jenny carried her hat into the kitchen and sat down at the table as before. The half-contemptuous smile had reappeared in her eyes; but her mouth was quite serious.

III

PA BLANCHARD had worked as a boy and man in a large iron foundry. He had been a very capable workman, and had received as the years went on the maximum amount (with overtime) to be earned by men doing his class of work. He had not been abstemious, and so he had spent a good deal of his earnings in what is in Kennington Park called 'pleasure'; but he had also possessed that common kind of sense which leads men to pay money into sick and benefit clubs. Accordingly, his wife's illness and burial had, as he had been in the habit of saying, 'cost him nothing.' They were paid by his societies. Similarly, when he had himself been attacked by the paralytic seizure which had wrecked his life, the societies had paid; and now, in addition to the pension allowed by his old employers, he received a weekly dole from the societies which brought his income up to fifty shillings a week. The pensions, of course, would cease upon his death; but so long as life was kept burning within him nothing could affect the amounts paid weekly into the Blanchard exchequer. Pa was fifty-seven, and normally would have had a respectable number of years before him; his wants were now few, and his days were carefully watched over by his daughters. He would continue to draw his pensions for several years yet, unless something unexpected happened to him. Meanwhile, therefore, his pipe was regularly filled and his old pewter tankard appeared at regular intervals, in order that Pa should feel as little as possible the change in his condition.

Mrs. Blanchard had been dead ten years. She

had been very much as Emmy now was, but a
great deal more cheerful. She had been plump
and fresh-coloured, and in spite of Pa Blanchard's
ways she had led a happy life. In the old days
there had been friends and neighbours, now all
lost in course of removals from one part of London to another, so that the girls were without
friends and knew intimately no women older
than themselves. Mrs. Blanchard, perhaps in
accord with her cheerfulness, had been a complacent selfish little woman, very neat and clean,
and disposed to keep her daughters in their
place. Jenny had been her favourite; and even
so early had the rivalry between them been
established. Besides this, Emmy had received
all the rebuffs needed to check in her the same
complacent selfishness that distinguished her
mother. She had been frustrate all along, first
by her mother, then by her mother's preference
for Jenny, finally (after a period during which
she dominated the household after her mother's
death) by Jenny herself. It was thus not upon
a pleasant record of personal success that Emmy
could look back, but rather upon a series of
chagrins of which each was the harder to bear
because of the history of its precursors. Emmy,
between eighteen and nineteen at the time of her
mother's death, had grasped her opportunity,
and had made the care of the household her lot.
She still bore, what was a very different reading
of her ambition, the cares of the household.

Jenny, as she grew up, had proved unruly; Pa Blanchard's illness had made home service compulsory; and so matters were like to remain indefinitely. Is it any wonder that Emmy was restive and unhappy as she saw her youth going and her horizons closing upon her with the passing of each year? If she had been wholly selfish that fact would have been enough to sour her temper. But another, emotionally more potent, fact produced in Emmy feelings of still greater stress. To that fact she had this evening given involuntary expression Now, how would she, how could she, handle her destiny? Jenny, shrewdly thinking as she sat with her father in the kitchen and heard Emmy open the front door, pondered deeply as to her sister's ability to turn to account her own sacrifice.

IV

WITHIN a moment, Alf Rylett appeared in the doorway of the kitchen, Emmy standing behind him until he moved forward, and then closing the door and leaning back against it. His first glance was in the direction of Jenny, who, however, did not rise as she would ordinarily have done. He glanced quickly at her face and from her face to her hands, so busily engaged in manipulating the materials from which she was to re-trim her hat. Then he looked at Pa Blanchard, whom he touched lightly and familiarly upon the shoulder. Alf was a rather squarely built young man of thirty, well under six feet, but not ungainly. He had a florid, reddish complexion, and his hair was of a common but unnamed colour, between brown and grey, curly and crisp. He was clean-shaven. Alf was obviously one who worked with his hands: in the little kitchen he appeared to stand upon the tips of his toes, in order that his walk might not be too noisy. That fact might have suggested either mere nervousness or a greater liking for life out of doors. When he walked it was as though he did it all of a piece, so that his shoulders moved as well as his legs. The habit was shown as he lunged forward to grip Jenny's hand. When he spoke he shouted, and he addressed Pa as a boy might have done who was not quite completely at his ease but who thought it necessary to pretend that he was so.

'Good evening, Mr. Blanchard!' he cried boisterously. 'Sitting by the fire, I see!'

Pa looked at him rather vacantly, apparently straining his memory in order to recognize the new-comer. It was plain that as a personal matter he had no immediate use for Alf Rylett; but he presently nodded his head.

'Sitting by the fire,' he confirmed. 'Getting a bit warm. It's cold to-night. Is there any noos, Alf Rylett?'

'Lots of it!' roared Alf, speaking as if it had been to a deaf man or a foreigner. 'They say this fire at Southwark means ten thousand pounds damage. Big factory there—gutted. Of course, no outside fire escapes. *As* usual. Fully insured, though. It'll cost them nothing. You can't help wondering what causes these fires when they're heavily insured. Eh? Blazing all night, it was. Twenty-five engines. Twenty-five, mind you! That shows it was pretty big, eh? I saw the red in the sky, myself. "Well," I thought to myself, "there's somebody stands to lose something," I thought. But the insurance companies are too wise to stand all the risk themselves. They share it out, you know. It's a mere flea-bite to them. And . . . a . . . well then there's a. . . . See, then there's a bigamy case.'

'Hey?' cried Pa sharply, brightening. 'What's that about?'

'Nothing much. Only a couple of skivvies. About ten pound three and fourpence between the pair of them. That was all he got.' Pa's interest visibly faded. He gurgled at his pipe and turned his face towards the mantelpiece. 'And . . . a . . . let's see, what else is there?' Alf racked his brains, puffing a little and arching his brows at the two girls, who seemed both to be listening, Emmy intently, as though she were repeating his words to herself. He went on: 'Train smash in Newcastle. Car went off the points. Eleven injured. Nobody killed. . . .'

'I don't call *that* much,' said Jenny, critically, with a pin in her mouth. 'Not much more than I told them an hour ago. He wants a murder, or

a divorce. All these little tin-pot accidents aren't
worth printing at all. What he wants is the
cross-examination of the man who found the
bones.'

It was comical to notice the change on Alf at
Jenny's interruption. From the painful concen-
tration upon memory which had brought his
eyebrows together there appeared in his expression the most delighted ease, a sort of archness
that made his face look healthy and honest.

'What's that you're doing?' he eagerly inquired, forsaking Pa, and obviously thankful at
having an opportunity to address Jenny directly.
He came over and stood by the table, in spite of
the physical effort which Emmy involuntarily
made to will that he should not do so. Emmy's
eyes grew tragic at his intimate, possessive manner in speaking to Jenny. 'I say!' continued Alf,
admiringly. 'A new hat, is it? Smart! Looks
absolutely A 1. Real West End style, isn't it?
Going to have some chiffong?'

'Sit down, Alf.' It was Emmy who spoke,
motioning him to a chair opposite to Pa. He
took it, his shoulder to Jenny, while Emmy sat
by the table, looking at him, her hands in her lap.

'How is he?' Alf asked, jerking his head at Pa.
'Perked up when I said "bigamy," didn't he!'

'He's been very good, I will say,' answered
Emmy. 'Been quiet all day. And he ate his supper as good as gold.' Jenny's smile and little
amused crouching of the shoulders caught her

eye. 'Well, so he did!' she insisted. Jenny took no notice. 'He's had his—mustn't say it, because he *always* hears that word, and it's not time for his evening. . . . Eight o'clock, he has it.'

'What's that?' said Alf, incautiously. 'Beer?'

'Beer!' cried Pa. 'Beer!' It was the cry of one who had been malignantly defrauded, a piteous wail.

'There!' said both the girls, simultaneously. Jenny added: 'Now you've done it!'

'All right, Pa! Not time yet!' But Emmy went to the kitchen cupboard as Pa continued to express the yearning that filled his aged heart.

'Sorry!' whispered Alf. 'Hold me hand out, naughty boy!'

'He's like a baby with his titty bottle,' explained Emmy. 'Now he'll be quiet again.'

Alf fidgeted a little. This contretemps had unnerved him. He was less sure of himself.

'Well,' he said at last, darkly. 'What I came in about . . . Quarter to eight, is it? By Jove, I'm late. That's telling Mr. Blanchard all the news. The fact is, I've got a couple of tickets for the theatre down the road—for this evening, I thought . . . erum. . . .'

'Oh, extravagance!' cried Jenny, gaily, dropping the pin from between her lips and looking in an amused flurry at Emmy's anguished face opposite. It was as though a chill had struck across the room, as though both Emmy's heart and her own had given a sharp twist at the shock.

'Ah, that's where you're wrong. That's what cleverness does for you.' Alf nodded his head deeply and reprovingly. 'Given to me, they were, by a pal o' mine who works at the theatre. They're for to-night. I thought——'

Jenny, with her heart beating, was stricken for an instant with panic. She bent her head lower, holding the rose against the side of her hat, watching it with a zealous eye, once again to test the effect. He thought she was coquetting, and leaned a little towards her. He would have been ready to touch her face teasingly with his forefinger.

'Oh,' Jenny exclaimed, with a hurried assumption of matter-of-fact ease suddenly ousting her panic. 'That's very good. So you thought you'd take *Emmy*! That was a very good boy!'

'I thought . . .' heavily stammered Alf, his eyes opened in a surprised way as he found himself thus headed off from his true intention. He stared blankly at Jenny, until she thought he looked like the bull on the hoardings who has 'heard that they want more.' Emmy stared at her also, quite unguardedly, a concentrated stare of agonised doubt and impatience. Emmy's face grew pinched and sallow at the unexpected strain upon her nerves.

'That was what you thought, wasn't it?' Jenny went on impudently, shooting a sideways glance at him that made Alf tame with helplessness. 'Poor old Em hasn't had a treat for ever so long. Do her good to go. You did mean that, didn't you?'

'I . . .' said Alf. 'I . . .' He was inclined for a moment to bluster. He looked curiously at Jenny's profile, judicial in its severity. Then some kind of tact got the better of his first impulse. 'Well, I thought *one* of you girls . . .' he said. 'Will you come, Em? Have to look sharp.'

'Really?' Emmy jumped up, her face scarlet and tears of joy in her eyes. She did not care how it had been arranged. Her pride was unaroused; the other thought, the triumph of the delicious moment, was overwhelming. Afterwards—ah, no no! She would not think. She was going. She was actually going. In a blur she saw their faces, their kind eyes. . . .

'Good boy!' cried Jenny. 'Buck up, Em, if you're going to change your dress. Seats! My word! How splendid!' She clapped her hands quickly, immediately again taking up her work so as to continue it. Into her eyes had come once more that strange expression of pitying contempt. Her white hands flashed in the wan light as she quickly threaded her needle and knotted the silk.

III. *ROWS*

AFTER Emmy had hurried out of the room to change her dress Alf stood, still apparently stupefied at the unscrupulous rush of Jenny's feminine tactics, rubbing his hand against the back of his head. He looked cautiously at Pa Blanchard, and from him back to the mysterious unknown who had so recently defeated his object. Alf may or may not have prepared some kind of set speech of invitation on his way to the house. Obviously it is a very difficult thing, where there are two girls in a family, to invite one of them and not the other to an evening's orgy. If it had not previously occurred to Alf to think of the difficulty quite as clearly as he was now being made to do, that must have been because he thought of Emmy as imbedded in domestic affairs. After all, damn it, as he was thinking; if you want one girl it is rotten luck to be fobbed off with another. Alf knew quite well the devastating phrase, at one time freely used as an irresistible quip (like 'There's hair' or 'That's all right, tell your mother; it'll be ninepence') by which one suggested disaster—'And that spoilt his evening.' The phrase was in his mind horrible to feel. Yet what could he have done in face of the direct assault? '*Must* be a gentleman.' He could hardly have said, before Emmy: 'No, it's *you* I want!' He began to think about Emmy. She was all right—a quiet little piece, and all that. But she hadn't got Jenny's cheek! That was it! Jenny had got the devil's own cheek, and this was an example of it. But this was an unwelcome example of it. He ruminated still further, until he found he was standing on one foot and rubbing the back of his head, just like any stage booby.

'Oh, damn!' he cried, putting his raised foot firmly on the ground and bringing his wandering fist down hard into the open palm of his other hand.

'Here, here!' protested Jenny, pretending to be scandalised. 'That's not the sort of language to use before Pa! He's not used to it. We're *awfully* careful what we say when Pa's here!'

'You're making a fool of me!' spluttered Alf, glaring at her. 'That's about the size of it!'

'What about your pa and ma?' she inquired, gibing at him. 'I've done nothing. Why don't you sit down? Of course you feel a fool, standing. I always do, when the manager sends for me. Think I'm going to get the sack.' She thought he was going to bellow at her: 'I hear they want more!' The mere notion of it made her smile, and Alf imagined that she was still laughing at her own manœuvre or at her impertinent jest.

'What did you do it for?' he asked, coming to the table.

'Cause it was all floppy. What did you think? Why, the girls all talk about me wearing it so long.'

'I'm not talking about that,' he said, in a new voice of exasperated determination. 'You know what I'm talking about. Oh, yes, you do! I'm talking about those tickets. And me. And you!'

Jenny's eyes contracted. She looked fixedly at her work. Her hands continued busy.

'Well, you're going to take Emmy, aren't you!' she prevaricated. 'You asked her to go.'

'No!' he said. 'I'm going with her, because she's said she'll go. But it was you that asked her.'

'Did I? How could I? They weren't mine. You're a man. You brought the tickets. You asked her yourself.' Jenny shook her head. 'Oh, no, Alf Rylett. You mustn't blame me. Take my advice, my boy. You be very glad Emmy's going. If you mean me, I should have said "No," because I've got to do this hat. Emmy's going to-night. You'll enjoy yourself far more.'

'Oh——!' He did not use an oath, but it was implied. 'What did you do it for? Didn't you want to come yourself? Now, look here, Jenny: I want to know what's going on. You've always come with me before.' He glared at her in perplexity, puzzled to the depths of his intelligence by a problem beyond its range. Women had always been reported to him as a mystery; but he had never heeded.

'It's Emmy's turn, then,' Jenny went on. She could not resist the display of a sisterly magnanimity, although it was not the true magnanimity, and in fact had no relation to the truth. 'Poor old Em gets stuck in here day after day,' she pleaded. 'She's always with Pa till he thinks she's a fixture. Well, why shouldn't she have a little pleasure? You get her some chocs . . . at that shop. . . . *You* know. It'll be the treat of her life. She'll be as grateful to you for it. . . . Oh, I'm very glad she's got the chance of going. It'll keep her happy for days!' Jenny, trying with all her might to set the affair straight and satisfy everybody, was appealing to his vanity to salve his vanity. Alf saw himself recorded as a public benefactor. He perceived the true sublimity of altruism.

'Yes,' he said, doggedly, recovering himself and becoming a man, becoming Alf Rylett, once again. 'That's all bally fine. Sounds well as you put it; but you knew as well as I did that I came to take *you*. I say nothing against Em. She's a good sort; but——'

Jenny suddenly kindled. He had never seen her so fine.

'She's the best sort!' she said, with animation. 'And don't you forget it, Alf. Me—why, I'm as selfish as . . . as *dirt* beside her. Look a little closer, my lad. You'll see Em's worth two of me. Any day! You think yourself jolly lucky she's going with you. That's all I've got to say to you!'

She had pushed her work back, and was looking up at him with an air of excitement. She had really been moved by a generous impulse. Her indifference to Alf no longer counted. It was swept away by a feeling of loyalty to Emmy. The tale she had told, the plea she had advanced upon Emmy's behalf, if it had not influenced him, had sent a warm thrill of conviction through her own heart. When she came thus to feel deeply she knew as if by instinct that Emmy, irritable unsatisfied Emmy, was as much superior to Alf as she herself was superior to him. A wave of arrogance swept her. Because he was a man, and therefore so delectable in the lives of two lonely girls, he was basely sure of his power to choose from among them at will. He had no such power at that moment, in Jenny's mind. He was the clay, for Emmy or herself to mould to their own advantage.

'You can think yourself *jolly* lucky, my lad!' she repeated. 'I can tell you that much!'

II

JENNY leant back in her chair exhausted by her excitement. Alf reached round for the chair he had left, and brought it to the table. He sat down, his elbows on the table and his hands clasped; and he looked directly at Jenny as though he were determined to explode this false bubble of misunderstanding which she was sedulously creating. As he looked at her, with his

face made keen by the strength of his resolve,
Jenny felt her heart turn to water. She was
physically afraid of him, not because he had any
power to move her, but because in sheer bullock-
like strength he was too much for her, as in
tenacity he had equally an advantage. As a
skirmisher, or in guerilla warfare, in which she
might always retire to a hidden fastness, baffling
pursuers by innumerable ruses and doublings,
Jenny could hold her own. On the plain, in face
of superior strength, she had not the solid force
needed to resist strong will and clear issues. Alf
looked steadily at her, his reddish cheeks more
red, his obstinate mouth more obstinate, so that
she could imagine the bones of his jaws cracking
with his determination.

'It won't do, Jen,' he said. 'And you know it.'

Jenny wavered. Her eyes flinched from the
necessary task of facing him down. Where
women of more breeding have immeasurable
resources of tradition behind them, to quell any
such inquisition, she was by training defenceless.
She had plenty of pluck, plenty of adroitness;
but she could only play the sex game with Alf
very crudely because he was not fine enough to
be diverted by such finesses as she could employ.
All Jenny could do was to play for safety in the
passage of time. If she could beat him off until
Emmy returned she could be safe for to-night;
and if she were safe now—anything might happen another day to bring about her liberation.

'Bullying won't do, I grant that,' she retorted defiantly. 'You needn't think it will.' She jerked her head.

'We're going to have this out,' Alf went on. Jenny darted a look of entreaty at the kicking clock which lay so helplessly upon its side. If only the clock would come to her aid, forgetting the episode of the tea-cosy!

'Take you all your time,' she said swiftly. 'Why, the theatre's all full by now. The people are all in. They're tuning up for the overture. Look at it!' She pointed a wavering finger at the clock.

'We're going to have this out—now!' repeated Alf. 'You know why I brought the tickets here. It was because I wanted to take *you*. It's no good denying it. That's enough. Somehow—I don't know why—you don't want to go; and while I'm not looking you shove old Em on to me.'

'That's what you say,' Jenny protested. Alf took no notice of her interruption. He doggedly proceeded.

'As I say, Em's all right enough. No fault to find with her.. But she's not you. And it's you I wanted. Now, if I take her——'

'You'll enjoy it very much,' she weakly asserted. 'Ever so much. Besides, Alf,'—she began to appeal to him, in an attempt to wheedle—'Em's a real good sort . . . You don't know half the things . . .'

'I know all about Em. I don't need you to

tell me what she is. I can see for myself.' Alf
rocked a little with an ominous obstinacy. His
eyes were fixed upon her with an unwinking
stare. It was as though, having delivered a blow
with the full weight of party bias, he were desir-
ing her to take a common-sense view of a vehement political issue.

'What can you see?' With a feeble dash of
spirit, Jenny had attempted tactical flight. The
sense of it made her feel as she had done, as a
little girl, in playing touch; when, with a swerve,
she had striven to elude the pursuer. So tense
were her nerves on such occasions that she
turned what is called 'goosey' with the feel of the
evaded fingers.

Alf rolled his head again, slightly losing his
temper at the inconvenient question, which, if
he had tried to answer it, might have diverted
him from the stern chase upon which he was
engaged. The sense of that made him doubly
resolved upon sticking to the point.

'Oh, never you mind,' he said, stubbornly.
'Quite enough of that. Now the question is—
and it's a fair one,—why did you shove Em on to
me?'

'I didn't! You did it yourself!'

'Well, that's a flat lie!' he cried, slapping the
table in a sudden fury, and glaring at her.
'That's what that is.'

Jenny crimsoned. It made the words no better
that Alf had spoken truly. She was deeply

offended. They were both now sparkling with temper, restless with it, and Jenny's teeth showing.

'I'm a liar, am I!' she exclaimed. 'Well, you can just lump it, then. I shan't say another word. Not if you call me a liar. You've come here . . .' Her breath caught, and for a second she could not speak. 'You've come here *kindly* to let us lick your boots, I suppose. Is that it? Well, we're not going to do it. We never have, and we never will. Never! It's a drop for you, you think, to take Emmy out. A bit of kindness on your part. She's not up to West End style. That it? But you needn't think you're too good for her. There's no reason, I'm sure. You're not! . . . All because you're a man. Auch! I'm sick of the men! You think you've only got to whistle. Yes, you do! You think if you crook your little finger . . . Oh no, my lad. That's where you're wrong. You're making a big mistake there. We can look after ourselves, thank you! No chasing after the men! Pa's taught us that. We're not quite alone. We haven't got to take—we've neither of us got to take—whatever's offered to us . . . as you think. We've got Pa still!'

Her voice had risen. An unexpected interruption stopped the argument for the merest fraction of time.

'Aye,' said Pa. 'They've got their old Pa!' He had taken his pipe out of his mouth and was looking towards the combatants with an eye that for one instant seemed the eye of perfect comprehension. It frightened Jenny as much as it disconcerted Alf. It was to both of them, but especially to Alf, like the shock of a cold sponge laid upon a heated brow.

'I never said you hadn't!' he sulkily said, and turned round to look amazedly at Pa. But Pa had subsided once more, and was drinking with mournful avidity from his tankard. Occupied with the tankard, Pa had neither eye nor thought for anything else. Alf resumed after the baffled pause. 'Yes. You've got him all right enough. . . .' Then: 'You're trying to turn it off with your monkey tricks!' he said suddenly. 'But I see what it is. I was a fool not to spot it at once. You've got some other fellow in tow. I'm not good enough for you any longer. Got no use for me yourself; but you don't mind turning me over to old Em. . . .' He shook his head. 'Well, I don't understand it,' he concluded miserably. 'I used to think you was straight, Jen.'

'I am!' It was a desperate cry, from her heart. Alf sighed.

'You're not playing the game, Jen old girl,' he said, more kindly, more thoughtfully. 'That's what's the matter. I don't know what it is, or what you're driving at; but that's what's wrong. What's the matter with me? Anything? I know I'm not much of a one to shout the odds about. I don't expect you to do that. Never did. But

I never played you a trick like this. What is it? What's the game you think you're playing?' When she did not answer his urgent and humble appeal he went on in another tone: 'I shall find out, mind you. It's going to stop here. I shall ask Emmy. I can trust her.'

'You *can't* ask her!' Jenny cried. It was wrung from her. 'You just dare to ask her. If she knew you hadn't meant to take her to-night, it ud break her heart. It would. There!' Her voice had now the ring of intense sincerity. She was not afraid, not defiant. She was a woman, defending another woman's pride.

Alf groaned. His cheeks became less ruddy. He looked quickly at the door, losing confidence.

'No: I don't know what it is,' he said again. 'I don't understand it.' He sat, biting his under lip, miserably undetermined. His grim front had disappeared. He was, from the conquering hero, become a crestfallen young man. He could not be passionate with Pa there. He felt that if only she were in his arms she could not be untruthful, could not resist him at all; but with the table between them she was safe from any attack. He was powerless. And he could not say he loved her. He would never be able to bring himself to say that to any woman. A woman might ask him if he loved her, and he would awkwardly answer that of course he did; but it was not in his nature to proclaim the fact in so many words. He had not the fluency, the dramatic sense, the imaginative power to sink and to forget his own self-consciousness. And so Jenny had won that battle —not gloriously, but through the sheer mischance of circumstances. Alf was beaten, and Jenny understood it.

'Don't *think* about me,' she whispered, in a quick pity. Alf still shook his head, reproachfully eyeing her with the old bull-like concern. 'I'm not worth thinking about. I'm only a beast. And you say you can trust Emmy. . . . She's ever so . . .'

'Ah, but she can't make me mad like you do!' he said simply. 'Jen, will you come another night . . . Do!' He was beseeching her, his hands stretched towards her across the table, as near to making love as he would ever be. It was his last faint hope for the changing of her heart towards him. But Jenny slowly shook her head from side to side, a judge refusing the prisoner's final desperate entreaties.

'No,' she said. 'It's no good, Alf. It'll never be any good as long as I live.'

III

ALF put out his hand and covered Jenny's hand with it; and the hand he held, after a swift movement, remained closely imprisoned. And just at that moment, when the two were striving for mastery, the door opened and Emmy came back into the room. She was fully dressed for going out, her face charmingly set off by the hat she had offered earlier to Jenny, her eyes alight with happiness, her whole bearing unutterably changed.

'*Now* who's waiting!' she demanded; and at the extraordinary sight before her she drew a quick breath, paling. It did not matter that the clinging hands were instantly apart, or that Alf rose hurriedly to meet her. 'What's that?' she asked, in a trembling tone. 'What are you doing?' As though she felt sick and faint she sat sharply down upon her old chair near the door. Jenny rallied.

'Only a kid's game,' she said. 'Nothing at all.' Alf said nothing, looking at neither girl. Emmy tried to speak again; but at first the words would not come. Finally she went on, with dreadful understanding.

'Didn't you want to take me, Alf? Did you want her to go?'

It was as though her short absence, perhaps even the change of costume, had worked a curious and cognate change in her mind. Perhaps it was that in her flushed happiness she had forgotten to be suspicious, or had blindly misread the meanings of the earlier colloquy, as a result of which the invitation had been given.

'Don't be so silly!' quickly cried Jenny. 'Of course he wanted you to go!'

'Alf!' Emmy's eyes were fixed upon him with a look of urgent entreaty. She looked at Alf with all the love, all the extraordinary intimate confidence with which women of her class do so generally regard the men they love, ready to yield judgment itself to his decision. When he did not answer, but stood still before them like a red-faced boy, staring down at the floor, she seemed to shudder, and began despairingly to unfasten the buttons of her thick coat. Jenny darted up and ran to check the process.

'Don't be a fool!' she breathed. 'Like that! You've got no time for a scene.' Turning to Alf, she motioned him with a swift gesture to the door. 'Look sharp!' she cried.

'I'm not going!' Emmy struggled with Jenny's restraining hands. 'It's no good fussing me, Jenny. . . . I'm not going. He can take who he likes. But it's not me.'

Alf and Jenny exchanged angry glances, each bitterly blaming the other.

'Em!' Jenny shouted. 'You're mad!'

'No, I'm not. Let me go! Let me go! He didn't want me to go. He wanted you. Oh, I knew it. I was a fool to think he wanted me.' Then, looking with a sort of crazed disdain at Jenny, she said coolly, 'Well, how is it you're not ready? Don't you see your *substitute*'s waiting? Your *land* lover!'

'Land!' cried Alf. 'Land! A sailor!' He flushed deeply, raising his arms a little as if to ward off some further revelation. Jenny, desperate, had her hands higher than her head, protestingly quelling the scene. In a loud voice she checked them.

'Do . . . not . . . be . . . fools!' she cried. 'What's all the fuss about? Simply because Alf's a born booby, standing there like a fool! I can't go. I wouldn't go—even if he wanted me. But he wants you!' She again seized Emmy, delaying once more Emmy's mechanical unfastening of the big buttons of her coat. 'Alf! Get your coat. Get her out of the house! I never heard such rubbish! Alf, say . . . tell her you meant her to go! Say it wasn't me!'

'I shouldn't believe him,' Emmy said, clearly. 'I know I saw him holding your hand.'

Jenny laughed hysterically.

'What a fuss!' she exclaimed. 'He's doing palmistry—reading it. All about . . . what's going to happen to me. Wasn't it, Alf!'

Emmy disregarded her, watching Alf's too-transparent uneasiness.

'You always *were* a little lying beast,' she said, venomously. 'A trickster.'

'You see?' Jenny said, defiantly to Alf. 'What my own sister says?'

'So you were. With your *sailor*. . . . And playing the fool with Alf!' Emmy's voice rose. 'You always were . . . I wonder Alf's never seen it long ago. . . .'

At this moment, with electrifying suddenness, Pa put down his tankard.

'What, ain't you gone yet?' he trembled. 'I thought you was going out!'

'How did he know?' They all looked sharply

at one another, sobered. So, for one instant, they stood, incapable of giving any explanation to the meekly inquiring old man who had disturbed their quarrel. Alf, so helpless before the girls, was steeled by the interruption. He took two steps towards Emmy.

'We'll have this out later on,' he said. 'Meanwhile . . . Come on, Em! It's just on eight. Come along, there's a good girl!' He stooped, took her hands, and drew her to her feet. Then, with uncommon tenderness, he re-buttoned her coat, and, with one arm about her, led Emmy to the door. She pressed back, but it was against him, within the magic circle of his arm, suddenly deliriously happy.

Jenny, still panting, stood as she had stood for the last few minutes, and watched their departure. She heard the front door close as they left the house; and with shaky steps went and slammed the door of the kitchen. Trembling violently she leant against the door, as Emmy had done earlier. For a moment she could not speak, could not think or feel; and only as a clock in the neighbourhood solemnly recorded the eighth hour did she choke down a little sob, and say with the ghost of her bereaved irony:

'That's *done* it!'

IV. *THE WISH*

WAITING until she had a little recovered her self-control, Jenny presently moved from the door to the
fireplace, and proceeded methodically to put
coals on the fire. She was still shaking slightly,
and the corners of her mouth were uncontrollably twitching with alternate smiles and other
raiding emotions; so that she did not yet feel in
a fit state to meet Pa's scrutiny. He might be the
old fool he sometimes appeared to be; and, in-
conveniently, he might not. Just because she did
not want him to be particularly bright it was
quite probable that he would have a flourish of
brilliance. That is as it occasionally happens, in
the dullest of mortals. So Jenny was some time
in attending to the fire, until she supposed that
any undue redness of cheek might be imagined
to have been occasioned by her strenuous activi-
ties. She then straightened herself and looked
down at Pa with a curious mixture of protective-
ness and anxiety.

'Pleased with yourself, aren't you?' she inquired, more to make conversation which might
engage the ancient mind in ruminant pastime
than to begin any series of inquiries into Pa's
mental states.

'Eh, Jenny?' said Pa, staring back at her.

'Ain't you gone out? Is it Emmy that's gone out? What did that fool Alf Rylett want? He was shouting. . . . I heard him.'

'Yes, Pa; but you shouldn't have listened,' rebuked Jenny, with a fine colour.

Pa shook his shaggy head. He felt cunningly for his empty tankard, hoping that it had been refilled by his benevolent genius. It was not until the full measure of his disappointment had been revealed that he answered her.

'I wasn't listening,' he quavered. 'I didn't hear what he said. . . . Did Emmy go out with him?'

'Yes, Pa. To the theatre. Alf brought tickets. Tickets! Tickets for seats. . . . Oh, dear! *Why* can't you understand! Didn't have to pay at the door. . . .'

Pa suddenly understood.

'Oh ah!' he said. 'Didn't have to pay. . . .' There was a pause. 'That's like Alf Rylett,' presently added Pa. Jenny sat looking at him in consternation at such an uncharitable remark.

'It's not!' she cried. 'I never *knew* you were such a wicked old man!'

Pa gave an antediluvian chuckle that sounded like a magical and appalling rattle from the inner recesses of his person. He was getting brighter and brighter, as the stars appear to do when the darkness deepens.

'See,' he proceeded. 'Did Alf say there was any noos?' He admitted an uncertainty. Furtively he looked at her, suspecting all the time that memory had betrayed him; but in his ancient way continuing to trust to Magic.

'Well, you didn't seem to think much of what he *did* bring. But I'll tell you a bit of news, Pa. And that is, that you've got a pair of the rummiest daughters I ever struck!'

Pa looked out from beneath his bushy grey eyebrows, resembling a worn and dilapidated perversion of Whistler's portrait of Carlyle. His eyelids seemed to work as he brooded upon her announcement. It was as though, together, these two explored the Blanchard archives for confirmation of Jenny's sweeping statement. The Blanchards of several generations might have been imagined as flitting across a fantastic horizon, keening for their withered laurels, thrown into the shades by these brighter eccentrics. It was, or it might have been, a fascinating speculation. But Pa did not indulge this antique vein for very long. The moment and its concrete images beguiled him back to the daughter before him and the daughter who was engaged in an unexpected emotional treat. He said:

'I know,' and gave a wide grin that showed the gaps in his teeth as nothing else could have done—not even the profoundest yawn. Jenny was stunned by this evidence of brightness in her parent.

'Well, you're a caution!' she cried. 'And to think of you sitting there saying it! And I reckon they've got a pretty rummy old Pa—if the truth was only known.'

Pa's grin, if possible, stretched wider. Again that terrible chuckle, which suggested a derangement of his internal parts, or the running-down of an overworked clock, wheezed across the startled air.

'Maybe,' Pa said, with some unpardonable complacency. 'Maybe.'

'Bless my soul!' exclaimed Jenny. She could not be sure, when his manner returned to one of vacancy, and when the kitchen was silent, whether Pa and she had really talked thus, or whether she had dreamed their talk. To her dying day she was never sure, for Pa certainly added nothing to the conversation thereafter. Was it real? Or had her too excited brain played her a trick? Jenny pinched herself. It was like a fairy tale, in which cats talk and little birds humanly sing, or the tiniest of fairies appear from behind clocks or from within flower-pots. She looked at Pa with fresh awe. There was no knowing where you had him! He had the interest, for her, of one returned by miracle from other regions, gifted with preposterous knowledges. . . . He became at this instant fabulous, like Rip Van Winkle, or the Sleeping Beauty . . . or the White Cat. . . .

In her perplexity Jenny fell once more into a kind of dream, an argumentative dream. She went back over the earlier rows, re-living them, exaggerating unconsciously the noble unselfishness of her own acts and the pointed effectiveness of her speeches, until the scenes were transformed. They now appeared in other hues, in other fashionings. This is what volatile minds are able to do with all recent happenings whatsoever, recasting them in form altogether more exquisite than the crude realities. The chiaroscuro of their experiences is thus so constantly changing and recomposing that—whatever the apparent result of the scene in fact—the dreamer is in retrospect always victor, in the heroic limelight. With Jenny this was a mood, not a preoccupation; but when she had been moved or excited beyond the ordinary she often did tend to put matters in a fresh aspect, more palatable to her self-love, and more picturesque in detail than the actual happening. That is one of the advantages of the rapidly-working brain, that its power of improvisation is, in solitude, very constant and reassuring. It is as though such a brain, upon this more strictly personal side, were a commonwealth of little cell-building microbes. The chief microbe comes, like the engineer, to estimate the damage to one's *amour propre* and to devise means of repair. He then summons all his necessary workmen, who are tiny self-loves and ancient praises and habitual complacencies and the staircase words of which one thinks too late for use in the scene itself; and with their help he restores that proportion without which the human being cannot maintain his self-respect. Jenny was like the British type as recorded in legend; being beaten, she never admitted it; but even, five minutes later, through the adroitness of her special engineer and his handymen, would be able quite seriously to demonstrate a victory to herself.

Defeat? Never! How Alf and Emmy shrank now before her increasing skill in argument. How were they shattered! How inept were their feeblenesses! How splendid Jenny had been in act, in motive, in speech, in performance!

'Er, yes!' Jenny said, beginning to ridicule her own highly coloured picture. 'Well, it was *something* like that!' She had too much sense of the ridiculous to maintain for long unquestioned the heroic vein as natural to her own actions. More justly, she resumed her consideration of the scenes, pondering over them in their nakedness and their meanings, trying to see how all these stupid little feelings had burst their way from overcharged hearts, and how each word counted as part of the mosaic of misunderstanding that had been composed.

'Oh, blow!' Jenny impatiently ejaculated, with a sinking heart at the thought of any sequel. A sequel there was bound to be—however muffled. It did not rest with her. There were Emmy and Alf, both alike burning with the wish to avenge themselves—upon her! If only she could disappear—just drop out altogether, like a

man overboard at night in a storm; and leave
Emmy and Alf to settle together their own
trouble. She couldn't drop out; nobody could,
without dying, though they might often wish to
do so; and even then their bodies were the only
things that were gone, because for a long time
they stubbornly survived in memory. No: she
couldn't drop out. There was no chance of it.
She was caught in the web of life; not alone, but
a single small thing caught in the general mix-
up of actions and inter-actions. She had just to
go on as she was doing, waking up each morning
after the events and taking her old place in the
world; and in this instance she would have,
somehow, to smooth matters over when the
excitements and agitations of the evening were
past. It would be terribly difficult. She could
not yet see a clear course. If only Emmy didn't
live in the same house! If only, by throwing Alf
over as far as concerned herself, she could at the
same time throw him into Emmy's waiting arms.
Why couldn't everybody be sensible? If only
they could all be sensible for half an hour everything could be arranged and happiness could be
made real for each of them. No: misunderstand-
ings were bound to come, angers and jealousies,
conflicting desires, stupid suspicions. . . . Jenny
fidgeted in her chair and eyed Pa with a sort of
vicarious hostility. Why, even that old man was
a complication! Nay, he was the worst thing of
all! But for him, she *could* drop out! There was

no getting away from him! He was as much permanently there as the chair upon which he was drowsing. She saw him as an incubus. And then Emmy being so fussy! Standing on her dignity when she'd give her soul for happiness! And then Alf being so . . . What was Alf? Well, Alf was stupid. That was the word for Alf. He was stupid. As stupid as any stupid member of his immeasurably stupid sex could be!

'Great booby!' muttered Jenny. Why, look at the way he had behaved when Emmy had come into the room. It wasn't honesty, mind you; because he could tell any old lie when he wanted to. It was just funk. He hadn't known where to look, or what to say. Too slow, he was, to think of anything. What could you do with a man like that? Oh, what stupids men were! She expected that Alf would feel very fine and noble as he walked old Em along to the theatre—and afterwards, when the evening was over and he had gone off in a cloud of glory. He would think it all over and come solemnly to the conclusion that the reason for his mumbling stupidity, his toeing and heeling, and all that idiotic speechlessness that set Emmy on her hind legs, was sheer love of the truth. He couldn't tell a lie— to a woman. That would be it. He would pretend that Jenny had chivvied him into taking Em, that he was too noble to refuse to take Em, or to let Em really see point-blank that he didn't want to take her; but when it came to the pinch he

hadn't been able to screw himself into the truly
noble attitude for such an act of self-sacrifice. He
had been speechless when a prompt lie, added to
the promptitude and exactitude of Jenny's lie,
would have saved the situation. Not Alf!

'I cannot tell a lie,' sneered Jenny. 'To a
woman. George Washington. I *don't* think!'

Yes; but then, said her secret complacency,
preening itself, and suggesting that possibly a
moment or two of satisfied pity might be at this
point in place, he'd really wanted to take Jenny.
He had taken the tickets because he had wanted
to be in Jenny's company for the evening. Not
Emmy's. There was all the difference. If you
wanted a cream bun and got fobbed off with a
scone! There was something in that. Jenny was
rather flattered by her happy figure. She even
excitedly giggled at the comparison of Emmy
with a scone. Jenny did not like scones. She
thought them stodgy. She had also that astound-
ing feminine love of cream buns which no true
man could ever acknowledge or understand. So
Emmy became a scone, with not too many cur-
rants in it. Jenny's fluent fancy was inclined to
dwell upon this notion. She a little lost sight of
Alf's grievance in her pleasure at the figures she
had drawn. Her mind was recalled with a jerk.
Now: what was it? Alf had wanted to take her—
Jenny. Right! He had taken Emmy. Right!
Because he had taken Emmy, he had a grievance.
Right! But against whom? Against Emmy?

Certainly not. Against himself? By no means. Against Jenny? A horribly exulting and yet nervously penitent little giggle shook Jenny at her inability to answer this point as she had answered the others. For Alf *had* a grievance against Jenny, and she knew it. No amount of ingenious thought could hoodwink her sense of honesty for more than a debater's five minutes. No. Alf had a grievance. Jenny could not, in strict privacy, deny the fact. She took refuge in a shameless piece of bluster.

'Well, after all!' she cried, 'he had the tickets given to him. It's not as though they *cost* him anything! So what's all the row about?'

II

THEREAFTER she began to think of Alf. He had taken her out several times—not as many times as Emmy imagined, because Emmy had thought about these excursions a great deal and not only magnified but multiplied them. Nevertheless, Alf had taken Jenny out several times. To a music hall once or twice; to the pictures, where they had sat and thrilled in cushioned darkness while acrobatic humans and grey-faced tragic creatures jerked and darted at top speed in and out of the most amazingly telescoped accidents and difficulties. And Alf had paid more than once, for all Pa said. It is true that Jenny had paid on her birthday for both of them; and that she had occasionally paid for herself upon an

impulse of sheer independence. But there had
been other times when Alf had really paid for
both of them. He had been very decent about it.
He had not tried any nonsense, because he was
not a flirtatious fellow. Well, it had been very
nice; and now it was all spoilt. It was spoilt
because of Emmy. Emmy had spoilt it by wanting Alf for herself. Ugh! thought Jenny. Em
had always been a jealous cat: if she had just
seen Alf somewhere she wouldn't have wanted
him. That was it! Em saw that Alf preferred
Jenny; she saw that Jenny went out with him.
And because she always wanted to do what
Jenny did, and always wanted what Jenny had
got, Em wanted to be taken out by Alf. Jenny,
with the cruel unerringness of an exasperated
woman, was piercing to Emmy's heart with fierce
lambent flashes of insight. And if Alf had taken
Em once or twice, and Jenny once or twice, not
wanting either one or the other, or not wanting
one of them more than the other, Em would have
been satisfied. It would have gone no further.
It would still have been sensible, without nonsense. But it wouldn't do for Em. So long as
Jenny was going out Emmy stayed at home. She
had said to herself: 'Why should Jenny go, and
not me . . . having all this pleasure?' That had
been the first stage—Jenny worked it all out.
First of all, it had been envy of Jenny's going out.
Then had come stage number two: 'Why should
Alf Rylett always take Jenny, and not me?'

That had been the first stage of jealousy of Alf. And the next time Alf took Jenny, Em had stayed at home, and thought herself sick about it, supposing that Alf and Jenny were happy and that she was unhappy, supposing they had all the fun, envying them the fun, hating them for having what she had not got, hating Jenny for monopolising Alf, hating Alf for monopolising Jenny; then, as she was a woman, hating Jenny for being a more pleasing woman than herself, and having her wounded jealousy moved into a strong craving for Alf, driven deeper and deeper into her heart by long-continued thought and frustrated desire. And so she had come to look upon herself as one defrauded by Jenny of pleasure—of happiness—of love—of Alf Rylett.

'And she calls it love!' thought Jenny bitterly. 'If that's love, I've got no use for it. Love's giving, not getting. I know that much. Love's giving yourself; wanting to give all you've got. It's got nothing at all to do with envy, or hating people, or being jealous. . . .' Then a swift feeling of pity darted through her, changing her thoughts, changing her every shade of the portrait of Emmy which she had been etching with her quick corrosive strokes of insight. 'Poor old Em!' she murmured. 'She's had a rotten time. I know she has. Let her have Alf if she wants. I don't want him. I don't want anybody . . . except . . .' She closed her eyes in the most fleeting vision. 'Nobody except just Keith. . . .'

Slowly Jenny raised her hand and pressed the back of her wrist to her lips, not kissing the wrist, but holding it against her lips so that they were forced hard back upon her teeth. She drew, presently, a deep breath, releasing her arm again and clasping her hands over her knees as she bent lower, staring at the glowing heart of the fire. Her lips were closely, seriously, set now; her eyes sorrowful. Alf and Emmy had receded from her attention as if they had been fantastic shadows. Pa, sitting holding his exhausted hubble-bubble, was as though he had no existence at all. Jenny was lost in memory and the painful aspirations of her own heart.

III

How the moments passed during her reverie she did not know. For her it seemed that time stood still while she recalled days that were beautified by distance, and imagined days that should be still to come, made to compensate for that long interval of dullness that pressed her each morning into acquiescence. She bent nearer to the fire, smiling to herself. The fire showing under the little door of the kitchener was a bright red glowing ash, the redness that came into her imagination when the words 'fire' or 'heat' were used— the red heart, burning and consuming itself in its passionate immolation. She loved the fire. It was to her the symbol of rapturous surrender, that feminine ideal that lay still deeper than her pride, locked in the most secret chamber of her nature.

And then, as the seconds ticked away, Jenny awoke from her dream and saw that the clock upon the mantelpiece said half-past eight. Half-past eight was what, in the Blanchard home, was called 'time.' When Pa was recalcitrant Jenny occasionally shouted very loud, with what might have appeared to some people an undesirable knowledge of customs, 'Act of Parliament, gentlemen, please'—which is a phrase sometimes used in clearing a public-house. To-night there was no need for her to do that. She had only to look at Pa, to take from his hand the almost empty pipe, to knock out the ashes, and to say:

'Time, Pa!' Obediently Pa held out his right hand and clutched in the other his sturdy walking-stick. Together they tottered into the bedroom, stood a moment while Jenny lighted the peep of gas which was Pa's guardian angel during the night, and then made their way to the bed. Pa sat upon the bed, like a child. Jenny took off Pa's collar and tie, and his coat and waistcoat; she took off his boots and his socks; she laid beside him the extraordinary faded scarlet night-gown in which Pa slept away the darkness. Then she left him to struggle out of his clothes as well as he could, which Pa did with a skill worthy of his best days. The cunning which replaces competence had shown him how the braces may be made to do their own work, how the shirt may with one hand be so manipulated as to be drawn swiftly over the head. . . . Pa was adept at undressing. He was in bed within five minutes, after a panting, exhausted interval during which he sat in a kind of trance, and was then proudly as usual knocking upon the floor with his walking-stick for Jenny to come and tuck him in for the night.

Jenny came, gave him a big kiss, and went back to the kitchen, where she resumed work upon her hat. It had lost its interest for her. She stitched quickly and roughly, not as one interested in needlework or careful for its own sake of the regularity of the stitch. Ordinarily she was accurate: to-night her attention was elsewhere. It had come back to the rows, because there is nothing either good or bad but thinking makes it ever so much more important than it really is. Loneliness with happy thoughts is perhaps an ideal state; but no torment could be greater than loneliness with thoughts that wound. Jenny's thoughts wounded her. The mood of complacency was gone: that of shame and discontent was upon her. Distress was uppermost in her mind—not the petulant wriggling of a spoilt child, but the sober consciousness of pain in herself and in others. In vain did Jenny give little gasps of annoyance, intended by her humour to disperse the clouds. The gasps and exclamations were unavailing. She was angry, chagrined, miserable. . . . At last she could bear the tension no longer, but threw down her work, rose, and walked impatiently about the kitchen.

'Oh, *do* shut up!' she cried to her insistent thoughts. 'Enough to drive anybody off their nut. And they're not worth it, either of them. Em's as stupid as she can be, thinking about herself. . . . And as for Alf—anybody'd think I'd tricked him. I haven't. I've gone out with him; but what's that? Lots of girls go out with fellows for months, and nobody expects them to marry. The girls may want it; but the fellows don't. They don't want to get settled down. And I don't blame them. Why is Alf different? I suppose it's me that's different. I'm not like other girls. . . .' That notion cheered her. 'No: I'm not like other girls. I want my bit of fun. I've never had any. And just because I don't want to settle down and have a lot of kids that mess the place to bits, of course I get hold of Alf! It's too bad! Why can't he choose the right sort of girl? Why can't he choose old Em? She's the sort that *does* want to get settled. She knows she'll have to buck up about it, too. She said I should get left. That's what she's afraid of, herself; only she's afraid of getting left on the shelf. . . . I wonder why it is the marrying men don't get hold of the marrying girls! They do, sometimes, I suppose. . . .' Jenny shrugged restlessly and stood looking at nothing. 'Oh, it's sickening! You can't do anything you like in this world. Nothing at all! You've always got to do what you *don't*

like. They say it's good for you. It's your
"duty." Who to? And who are "they," to say
such a thing. What are they after? Just to keep
people like me in their place—do as you're told.
Well, I'm not going to do as I'm told. They can
lump it! That's what they can do. What does
it matter—what happens to me? I'm me, aren't
I? Got a right to live, haven't I? Why should I
be somebody's servant all my life? I *won't*! If
Alf doesn't want to marry Emmy, he can go and
whistle somewhere else. There's plenty of girls
who'd jump at him. But just because I don't,
he'll worry me to death. If I was to be all over
him—see Alf sheer off! He'd think there was
something funny about me. Well, there is! I'm
Jenny Blanchard; and I'm going to keep Jenny
Blanchard. If I've got no right to live, then
nobody's got any right to keep me from living.
If there's no rights, other people haven't got any
more than I have. They can't make me do anything—by any right they've got. People—
managing people—think that because there
isn't a corner of the earth they haven't collared
they can tell you what you've got to do. Give
you a ticket and a number, get up at six, eat
so much a day, have six children, do what
you're told. That may do for some people; but
it's slavery. And I'm not going to do it. See!'
She began to shout in her excited indignation.
'See!' she cried again. 'Just because I'm poor,
I'm to do what I'm told. They seem to think

that because they like to do what they're told,
everybody ought to be the same. They're afraid.
They're afraid of themselves—afraid of being
left alone in the dark. They think everybody
ought to be afraid—in case anybody should find
out that they're cowards! But I'm not afraid,
and I'm not going to do what I'm told. . . . I
wont!'

In a frenzy she walked about the room, her
eyes glittering, her face flushed with tumultuous
anger. This was her defiance to life. She had
been made into a rebel through long years in
which she had unconsciously measured herself
with others. Because she was a human being,
Jenny thought she had a right to govern her own
actions. With a whole priesthood against her,
Jenny was a rebel against the world as it appeared to her—a crushing, numerically overwhelming pressure that would rob her of her one
spiritual reality—the sense of personal freedom.

'Oh, I can't stand it!' she said bitterly. 'I shall
go mad! And Em taking it all in, and ready to
have Alf's foot on her neck for life. And Alf
ready to have Em chained to his foot for life.
The fools! Why, I wouldn't . . . not even to
Keith. . . . No, I wouldn't. . . . Fancy being
boxed up and pretending I like it—just because
other people say they like it. Do as you're told.
Do like other people. All be the same—a sticky
mass of silly fools doing as they're told! All for
a bit of bread, because somebody's bagged the

flour for ever! And what's the good of it? If it was any good—but it's no good at all! And they go on doing it because they're cowards! Cowards, that's what they all are. Well, I'm not like that!'

Exhausted, Jenny sat down again; but she could not keep still. Her feet would not remain quietly in the place she, as the governing intelligence, commanded. They too were rebels, nervous rebels, controlled by forces still stronger than the governing intelligence. She felt trapped, impotent, as though her hands were tied; as though only her whirling thoughts were unfettered. Again she took up the hat, but her hands so trembled that she could not hold the needle steady. It made fierce jabs into the hat. Stormily unhappy she once more threw the work down. Her lips trembled. She burst into bitter tears, sobbing as though her heart were breaking. Her whole body was shaken with the deep and passionate sobs that echoed her despair.

IV

PRESENTLY, when she grew calmer, Jenny wiped her eyes, her face quite pale and her hands still convulsively trembling. She was worn out by the stress of the evening, by the vehemence of her rebellious feelings. When she again spoke to herself it was in a shamed, giggling way that nobody but Emmy had heard from her since the days of childhood. She gave a long sigh, looking through the blur at that clear glow from beneath the iron door of the kitchen grate. Miserably she refused to think again. She was half sick of thoughts that tore at her nerves and lacerated her heart. To herself Jenny felt that it was no good—crying was no good, thinking was no good, loving and sympathising and giving kindness—all these things were in this mood as useless as one another. There was nothing in life but the endless sacrifice of human spirit.

'Oh!' she groaned passionately. 'If only something would happen. I don't care *what*! But something . . . something new . . . exciting. Something with a bite in it!'

She stared at the kicking clock, which every now and again seemed to have a spasm of distaste for its steady record of the fleeting seconds. 'Wound up to go all day!' she thought, comparing the clock with herself in an angry impatience.

And then, as if it came in answer to her poignant wish for some untoward happening, there was a quick double knock at the front door of the Blanchards' dwelling, and a sharp whirring ring at the push-bell below the knocker. The sounds seemed to go violently through and through the little house in rapid waves of vibrant noise.

Part Two

NIGHT

V. *THE ADVENTURE*

I

SO unexpected was this interruption of her loneliness that Jenny was for an instant stupefied. She took one step, and then paused, dread firmly in her mind, paralysing her. What could it be? She could not have been more frightened if the sound had been the turning of a key in the lock. Were they back already? Had her hope been spoiled by some accident? Surely not. It was twenty minutes to nine. They were safe in the theatre by now. Oh, she was afraid! She was alone in the house—worse than alone! Jenny cowered. She felt she could not answer the summons. Tick-tick-tick said the clock, striking across the silences. Again Jenny made a step forward. Then, terrifying her, the noise began once more—the thunderous knock, the ping-ping-ping-whir of the bell. . . .

Wrenching her mind away from apprehensiveness she moved quickly to the kitchen door and into the dimly-lighted dowdy passage-way. Somewhere beyond the gas flicker and the hat-stand lay—what? With all her determination she pushed forward, almost running to the door. Her hand hovered over the little knob of the lock: only horror of a renewal of that dreadful sound prompted her to open the door quickly She peered into the darkness, faintly silhouetted against the wavering light of the gas. A man stood there.

'Evening, miss,' said the man. 'Miss Jenny Blanchard?'

She could see there something white. He was holding it out to her. A letter!

'For me,' she asked, her voice still unsteady. She took the letter, a large square envelope. Mechanically she thanked the man, puzzling at the letter. From whom could a letter be brought to her?

'There's an answer,' she heard. It came from ever so far away, in the dim distance beyond her vague wonderings. Jenny was lost, submerged in the sensations through which she had passed during the evening. She was quite unlike herself, timid and fearful, a frightened girl alone in an unhappy house.

'Wait a bit!' she said. 'Will you wait there?'

'Yes,' answered the man, startlingly enough. 'I've got the car here.'

The car! What did it mean? She caught now, as her eyes were more used to the darkness, the sheen of light upon a peaked cap such as would be worn by a chauffeur. It filled her mind that this man was in uniform. But if so, why? From whom should the letter come? He had said 'Miss Jenny Blanchard.'

'You *did* say it was for me? I'll take it inside. . . .' She left the door unfastened, but the man pulled it right to, so that the catch clicked.

Then Jenny held the letter up under the flame of the passage gas. She read there by this meagre light her own name, the address, written in a large hand, very bold, with a sharp sweeping stroke under all, such as a man of impetuous strength might make. There was a blue seal fastening the flap—a great pool of solid wax. Trembling so that she was hardly able to tear the envelope, Jenny returned to the kitchen, again scanning the address, the writing, the blue seal with its Minerva head. Still, in her perplexity, it seemed as though her task was first to guess the identity of the sender. Who could have written to her? It was unheard-of, a thing for wondering jest, if only her lips had been steady and her heart beating with normal pulsation. With a shrug she turned back from the seal to the address. She felt that some curious mistake had been made, that the letter was not for her at all, but for some other Jenny Blanchard, of whom she had never until now heard. Then, casting such a fantastic thought aside with another impatient effort, she tore the envelope, past the seal, in a ragged dash. Her first glance was at the signature. 'Yours always, KEITH.'

Keith! Jenny gave a sob and moved swiftly to the light. Her eyes were quite blurred with shining mist. She could not read the words. Keith! She could only murmur his name, holding the letter close against her.

II

'MY DEAR JENNY,' said the letter. 'Do you remember? I said I should write to you when I got back. Well, here I am. I can't come to you myself. I'm tied here by the leg, and mustn't leave for a moment. But you said you'd come to me. Will you? Do! If you can come, you'll be a most awful dear, and I shall be out of my wits with joy. Not really out of my wits. *Do* come, there's a dear good girl. It's my only chance, as I'm off again in the morning. The man who brings this note will bring you safely to me in the car, and will bring you quite safely home again. *Do* come! I'm longing to see you. I trust you to come. I will explain everything when we meet. Yours always, KEITH.'

A long sigh broke from Jenny's lips as she finished reading. She was transfigured. Gone was the defiant look, gone were the sharpnesses that earlier had appeared upon her face. A soft colour flooded her cheeks; her eyes shone. Come to him! She would go to the end of the world. . . . Keith! She said it aloud, in a voice that was rich with her deep feeling, magically transformed.

'Come to you, my dear!' said Jenny. 'As if you need ask!'

Then she remembered that Emmy was out, that she was left at home to look after her father, that to desert him would be a breach of trust.

Quickly her face paled, and her eyes became horror-laden. She was shaken by the conflict of love and love, love that was pity and love that was the overwhelming call of her nature. The letter fluttered from her fingers, swooping like a wounded bird to the ground, and lay unheeded at her feet.

III

'WHAT *shall* I do?' Nobody to turn to; no help from any hand. To stay was to give up the chance of happiness. To go—oh, she couldn't go! If Keith was tied, so was Jenny. Half demented, she left the letter where it had fallen, a white square upon the shabby rug. In a frenzy she wrung her hands. What could she do? It was a cry of despair that broke from her heart. She couldn't go, and Keith was waiting. That it should have happened upon this evening of all others! It was bitter! To send back a message, even though it be written with all her love, which still she must not express to Keith in case he should think her lightly won, would be to lose him for ever. He would never stand it. She saw his quick irritation, the imperious glance. . . . He was a king among men. She must go! Whatever the failure in trust, whatever the consequences, she must go. She couldn't go! Whatever the loss to herself, her place was here. Emmy would not have gone to the theatre if she had not known that Jenny would stay loyally there. It was too hard! The months, the long months during which Keith had not written, were upon her mind like a weariness. She had had no word from him, and the little photograph that he had laughingly offered had been her only consolation. Yes, well, why hadn't he written? Quickly her love urged his excuse. She might accuse him of having forgotten her, but to herself she explained and pardoned all. That was not for this moment. Keith was not in fault. It was this dreadful difficulty of occasion, binding her here when her heart was with him. To sit moping here by the fire when Keith called to her! Duty —the word was a mockery. 'They' would say she ought to stay. Hidden voices throbbed the same message into her consciousness. But every eager impulse, winged with love, bade her go. To whom was her heart given? To Pa? Pity . . . pity. . . . She pitied him, helpless at home. If anything happened to him? Nothing would happen. What could happen? Supposing she had gone to the chandler's shop: in those few minutes all might happen that could happen in all the hours she was away. Yet Emmy often ran out, leaving Pa alone. He was in bed, asleep; he would not awaken, and would continue to lie there at rest until morning. Supposing she had gone to bed—she would still be in the house; but in no position to look after Pa. He might die any night while they slept. It was only the idea of leaving him, the superstitious idea that just *be-*

cause she was not there something would happen. Suppose she didn't go; but sat in the kitchen for two hours and then went to bed. Would she ever forgive herself for letting slip the chance of happiness that had come direct from the clouds? Never! But if she went, and something *did* happen, would she ever in that event know self-content again in all the days of her life? Roughly she shouldered away her conscience, those throbbing urgencies that told her to stay. She was to give up everything for a fear? She was to let Keith go for ever? Jenny wrung her hands, drawing sobbing breaths in her distress.

Something made her pick the letter swiftly up and read it through a second time. So wild was the desire to go, that she began to whimper, kissing the letter again and again, holding it softly to her cold cheek. Keith! What did it matter? What did anything matter but her love? Was she never to know any happiness? Where, then, was her reward? A heavenly crown of martyrdom? What was the good of that? Who was the better for it? Passionately Jenny sobbed at such a mockery of her overwhelming impulse. 'They' hadn't such a problem to solve. 'They' didn't know what it was to have your whole nature craving for the thing denied. 'They' were cowards, enemies to freedom because they liked the music of their manacles! They could not understand what it was to love so that one adored the beloved. Not blood but water ran in their

veins! They didn't know. . . . They couldn't feel.
Jenny knew, Jenny felt; Jenny was racked with
the sweet passion that blinds the eyes to consequences. She *must* go! Wickedness might be her
nature: what then? It was a sweet wickedness.
It was her choice!

Jenny's glance fell upon the trimmed hat
which lay upon the table. Nothing but a cry
from her father could have prevented her from
taking it up and setting it upon her head. The
act was her defiance. She was determined. As
one deaf and blind she went out of the kitchen,
and to the hall-stand, fumbling there for her
hatpins. She pinned her hat as deliberately as
she might have done in leaving the house any
morning. Her pale face was set. She had flung
the gage. There remained only the acts con-
sequential. And of those, since they lay behind
the veil of night, who could now speak? Not
Jenny!

IV

THERE was still Pa. He was there like a secret,
lying snug in his warm bed, drowsily coaxing
sleep while Jenny planned a desertion. Even
when she was in the room, her chin grimly set
and her lips quivering, a shudder seemed to still
her heart. She was afraid. She could not forget
him. He lay there so quiet in the semi-darkness,
a long mound under the bedclothes; and she was
almost terrified at speaking to him because her

imagination was heightened by the sight of his dim outline. He was so helpless! Ah, if there had only been two Jennies, one to go, one to stay. The force of uncontrollable desire grappled with her pity. She still argued within herself, a weary echo of her earlier struggle. He would need nothing, she was sure. It would be for such a short time that she left him. He would hardly know she was not there. He would think she was in the kitchen. But if he needed her? If he called, if he knocked with his stick, and she did not come, he might be alarmed, or stubborn, and might try to find his way through the passage to the kitchen. If he fell! Her flesh crept as she imagined him helpless upon the floor, feebly struggling to rise. . . . It was of no use. She was bound to tell him. . . .

Jenny moved swiftly from the room, and returned with his nightly glass and jug of water. There could be nothing else that he would want during the night. It was all he ever had, and he would sleep until morning. She approached the bed on tiptoe.

'Pa,' she whispered. 'Are you awake?' He stirred, and looked out from the bedclothes, and she was fain to bend over him and kiss the tumbled hair. 'Pa, dear . . . I want to go out. I've got to go out. Will you be all right if I leave you? Sure? You'll be a good boy, and not move! I shall be back before Emmy, and you won't be lonely, or frightened—will you!' She exhorted him. 'See, I've *got* to go out; and if I can't leave you . . . You *are* awake, Pa?'

'Yes,' breathed Pa, half asleep. 'A good boy. Night, Jennie my dearie girl.'

She drew back from the bed, deeply breathing, and stole to the door. One last glance she took, at the room and at the bed, closed the door and stood irresolute for a moment in the passage. Then she whipped her coat from the peg and put it on. She took her key and opened the front door. Everything was black, except that upon the roofs opposite the rising moon cast a glittering surface of light, and the chimney pots made slanting broad markings upon the silvered slates. The road was quite quiet but for the purring of a motor, and she could now, as her eyes were clearer, observe the outline of a large car drawn to the left of the door. As the lock clicked behind her and as she went forward the side-lights of the motor blazed across her vision, blinding her again.

'Are you there?' she softly called.

'Yes, miss.' The man's deep voice came sharply out of the darkness, and he jumped down from his seat to open the door of the car. The action startled Jenny. Why had the man done that?

'Did you know I was coming?' she suddenly asked, drawing back with a sort of chill.

'Yes, miss,' said the man. Jenny caught her breath. She half turned away, like a shy horse

that fears the friendly hand. He had been sure
of her, then. Oh, that was a wretched thought!
She was shaken to the heart by such confidence.
He had been sure of her! There was a flash of
time in which she determined not to go; but it
passed with dreadful speed. Too late, now, to
draw back. Keith was waiting: he expected her!
The tears were in her eyes. She was more unhappy than she had been yet, and her heart was
like water.

The man still held open the door of the car.
The inside was warm and inviting. His hand was
upon her elbow; she was lost in the soft cushions,
and drowned in the sweet scent of the great nose-
gay of flowers which hung before her in a shining
holder. And the car was purring more loudly,
and moving, moving as a ship moves when it
glides so gently from the quay. Jenny covered
her face with her hands, which cooled her burning cheeks as if they had been ice. Slowly the
car nosed out of the road into the wider thorough-
fare. Her adventure had begun in earnest.
There was no drawing back now.

VI. *THE YACHT*

I

TO lie deep among cushions, and gently to ride out along streets and roads that she had so often tramped in every kind of weather, was enough to intoxicate Jenny. She heard the soft humming of the engine, and saw lamps and other vehicles flashing by, with a sense of effortless speed that was to her incomparable. If only she had been mentally at ease, and free from distraction, she would have enjoyed every instant of her journey. Even as it was, she could not restrain her eagerness as they overtook a tramcar, and the chauffeur honked his horn, and they glided nearer and nearer, and passed and seemed to leave the tram standing. Each time this was in process of happening Jenny gave a small excited chuckle, thinking of the speed, and the ease, and of how the people in the tram must feel at being defeated in the race. Every such encounter became a race, in which she pressed physically forward as if to urge her steed to the final effort. Never had Jenny been so eager for victory, so elated when its certainty was confirmed. It was worth while to live for such experience. How she envied her driver! With his steady hands upon the steering wheel. . . . Ah, he was like a sailor, like the sailor of romance, with the wind beating upon his face and his eyes ever-watchful. And under his hand the car rode splendidly to Keith.

Jenny closed her eyes. She could feel her heart, beating fast, and the blood heating her cheeks, reddening them. The blood hurt her, and her mouth seemed to hurt, too, because she had smiled so much. She lay back, thinking of Keith and of their meetings—so few, so long ago, so indescribably happy and beautiful. She always remembered him as he had been when first he had caught her eye, when he had stood so erect among other men who lounged by the sea, smoking and lolling at ease. He was different, as she was different. And she was going to him. How happy she was! And why did her breath come quickly and her heart sink? She could not bother to decide that question. She was too excited to do so. In all her life she had never known a moment of such breathless anticipation, of excitement which she believed was all happiness.

There was one other thought that Jenny shirked, and that went on nevertheless in spite of her inattention, plying and moulding somewhere deep below her thrilling joy. The thought was, that she must not show Keith that she loved him, because while she knew—she felt sure—that he loved her, she must not be the smallest fraction of time before him in confession. She was too proud for that. He would tell her that he loved her; and the spell would be broken. Her shyness would be gone; her bravado immediately unnecessary. But until then she must beware. It was as necessary to Keith's pride as to her own that he should win her. The Keith she loved would not care for a love too easily won. The consciousness of this whole issue was at work below her thoughts; and her thoughts, from joy and dread, to the discomfort of doubt, raced faster than the car, speedless and headlong. Among them were two that bitterly corroded. They were of Pa and Keith's confidence that she would come. Both were as poison in her mind.

II

AND then there came a curious sense that something had happened. The car stopped in darkness, and through the air there came in the huge tones of Big Ben the sound of a striking hour. It was nine o'clock. They were back at Westminster. Before her was the bridge, and above was the lighted face of the clock, like some faded sun. And the strokes rolled out in swelling waves that made the whole atmosphere feel sound-laden. The chauffeur had opened the door of the car, and was offering his free hand to help Jenny to step down to the ground.

'Are we *there*?' she asked in a bewildered way, as if she had been dreaming. 'How quick we've been!'

'Yes, miss. Mr. Redington's down the steps. You see them steps. Mr. Redington's down

there in the dinghy. Mind how you go, miss.
Hold tight to the rail. . . .' He closed the door of
the car and pointed to the steps.

The dinghy! Those stone steps to the black
water! Jenny was shaken by a shudder. The
horror of the water which had come upon her
earlier in the evening returned more intensely.
The strokes of the clock were the same, the darkness, the feeling of the sinister water rolling there
beneath the bridge, resistlessly carrying its bur-
dens to the sea. If Keith had not been there she
would have turned and run swiftly away, overcome by her fear. She timidly reached the steps,
and stopped, peering down through the dimness.
She put her foot forward so that it hung dubiously
beyond the edge of the pavement.

'What a coward!' she thought, violently, with
self-contempt. It drove her forward. And at
that moment she could see below, at the edge of
the lapping water, the outline of a small boat and
of a man who sat in it using the oars against the
force of the current so as to keep the boat always
near the steps. She heard a dear familiar voice
call out with a perfect shout of welcome:

'Jenny! Good girl! How are you! Come
along; be careful how you come. That's it. . . .
Six more, and then stop!' Jenny obeyed him—
she desired nothing else, and her doubtings were
driven away in a breath. She went quickly down.
The black water lapped and wattled against the
stone and the boat, and she saw Keith stand up,

drawing the dinghy against the steps and offering
her his hand. He had previously been holding
up a small lantern that gilded the brown mud
with a feeble colour and made the water look
like oil. 'Now!' he cried quickly. 'Step!' The
boat rocked, and Jenny crouched down upon the
narrow seat, aflame with rapture, but terrified of
the water. It was so near, so inescapably near.
The sense of its smooth softness, its yieldingness,
and the danger lurking beneath the flowing surface was acute. She tried more desperately to
sit exactly in the middle of the boat, so that she
should not overbalance it. She closed her eyes,
sitting very still, and heard the water saying
plup-plup-plup all round her, and she was afraid.
It meant soft death: she could not forget that.
Jenny could not swim. She was stricken between
terror and joy that overwhelmed her. Then:

'That's my boat,' Keith said, pointing. 'I say,
you *are* a sport to come!' Jenny saw lights shining
from the middle of the river, and could imagine
that a yacht lay there stubbornly resisting the
current of the flowing Thames.

III

CROUCHING still, she watched Keith bend to his
oars, driving the boat's nose beyond the shadowy
yacht because he knew that he must allow for the
current. Her eyes devoured him, and her heart
sang. Plup-plup-plup-plup said the water. The
oars plashed gently. Jenny saw the blackness

gliding beside her, thick and swift. They might go down down down in that black nothingness, and nobody would know of it. . . . The oars ground against the edge of the dinghy—wood against wood, grumbling and echoing upon the water. Behind everything she heard the roaring of London, and was aware of lights, moving and stationary, high above them. How low upon the water they were! It seemed to be on a level with the boat's edges. And how much alone they were, moving there in the darkness while the life of the city went on so far above. If the boat sank! Jenny shivered, for she knew that she would be drowned. She could imagine a white face under the river's surface, lanterns flashing, and then— nothing. It would be all another secret happening, a mystery, the work of a tragic instant; and Jenny Blanchard would be forgotten for ever, as if she had never been. It was a horrid sensation to her as she sat there, so near death.

And all the time that Jenny was mutely endur-ing these terrors they were slowly nearing the yacht, which grew taller as they approached, and more clearly outlined against the sky. The moon was beginning to catch all the buildings and to lighten the heavens. Far above, and very pale, were stars; but the sky was still murky, so that the river remained in darkness. They came alongside the yacht. Keith shipped his oars, caught hold of something which Jenny could not see; and the dinghy was borne round, away from the yacht's side. He half rose, catching with both his hands at an object projecting from the yacht, and hastily knotting a rope. Jenny saw a short ladder hanging over the side, and a lantern shining.

'There you are!' Keith cried. 'Up you go! It's quite steady. Hold the brass rail . . .'

After a second in which her knees were too weak to allow of her moving, Jenny conquered her tremors, rose unsteadily in the boat, and cast herself at the brass rail that Keith had indicated. To the hands that had been so tightly clasped together, steeling her, the rail was startlingly cold; but the touch of it nerved her, because it was firm. She felt the dinghy yield as she stepped from it, and she seemed for one instant to be hanging precariously in space above the terrifying waters. Then she was at the top of the ladder, ready for Keith's warning shout about the descent to the deck. She jumped down. She was aboard the yacht; and as she glanced around Keith was upon the deck beside her, catching her arm. Jenny's triumphant complacency was so great that she gave a tiny nervous laugh. She had not spoken at all until this moment: Keith had not heard her voice.

'Well!' said Jenny. '*That's* over!' And she gave an audible sigh of relief. 'Thank goodness!'

'And here you are!' Keith cried. 'Aboard the *Minerva.*'

IV

HE led her to a door, and down three steps. And then it seemed to Jenny as if Paradise burst upon her. She had never before seen such a room as this cabin. It was a room such as she had dreamed about in those ambitious imaginings of a wondrous future which had always been so vaguely irritating to Emmy. It seemed, partly because the ceiling was low, to be very spacious; the walls and ceiling were of a kind of dusky amber hue; a golden brown was everywhere the prevailing tint. The tiny curtains, the long settees into which one sank, the chairs, the shades of the mellow lights—all were of some variety of this delicate golden brown. In the middle of the cabin stood a square table; and on the table, arrayed in an exquisitely white tablecloth, was laid a wondrous meal. The table was laid for two: candles with amber shades made silver shine and glasses glitter. Upon a fruit-stand were peaches and nectarines; upon a tray she saw decanters; little dishes crowding the table bore mysterious things to eat such as Jenny had never before seen. Upon a side-table stood other dishes, a tray bearing coffee cups and ingredients for the provision of coffee, curious silver boxes. Everywhere she saw flowers similar to those which had been in the motor car. Under her feet was a carpet so thick that she felt her shoes must be hidden in its pile. And over all was this air of quiet expectancy which suggested that everything awaited her coming. Jenny gave a deep sigh, glanced quickly at Keith, who was watching her, and turned away, her breath catching. The contrast was too great: it made her unhappy. She looked down at her skirt, at her hands; she thought of her hat and her hidden shoes. She thought of Emmy, the bread and butter pudding, of Alf Rylett . . . of Pa lying at home in bed, alone in the house.

v

KEITH drew her forward slightly, until she came within the soft radiance of the cabin lights.

'I say, it *is* sporting of you to come!' he said. 'Let's have a look at you—do!'

They stood facing one another. Keith saw Jenny, tall and pale, looking thin in her shabby dress, but indescribably attractive and beautiful even in her new shyness. And Jenny saw the man she loved: her eyes were veiled, but they were unfathomably those of one deeply in love. She did not know how to hide the emotions with which she was so painfully struggling. Pride and joy in him; shyness and a sort of dread; hunger and reserve—Keith might have read them all, so plainly were they written. Yet her first words were wounded and defiant.

'The man . . . that man . . . He *knew* I was coming,' she said, in a voice of reproach. 'You were pretty sure I should come, you know.'

Keith said quietly:

'I *hoped* you would.' And then he lowered his eyes. She was disarmed, and they both knew.

Keith Redington was nearly six feet in height. He was thin, and even bony; but he was very toughly and strongly built, and his face was as clean and brown as that of any healthy man who travels far by sea. He was less dark than Jenny, and his hair was almost auburn, so rich a chestnut was it. His eyes were blue and heavily lashed; his hands were long and brown, with small freckles between the knuckles. He stood with incomparable ease, his hands and arms always ready, but in perfect repose. His lips, for he was clean-shaven, were keen and firm. His glance was fearless. As the phrase is, he looked every inch a sailor, born to challenge the winds and the waters. To Jenny, who knew only those men who show at once what they think or feel, his greater breeding made Keith appear inscrutable, as if he had belonged to a superior race. She could only smile at him, with parted lips, not at all the baffling lady of the mirror, or the contemptuous younger sister, or the daring franc-tireur of her little home at Kennington Park. Jenny Blanchard she remained, but the simple, eager Jenny to whom these other Jennies were but imperious moods.

'Well, I've come,' she said. 'But you needn't have been so sure.'

Keith gave an irrepressible grin. He motioned her to the table, shaking his head at her tone.

'Come and have some grub,' he said cheerfully. 'I was about as sure as you were. You
needn't worry about that, old sport. There's so
little time. Come and sit down; there's a good
girl. And presently I'll tell you all about it.'
He looked so charming as he spoke that Jenny
obediently smiled in return, and the light came
rushing into her eyes, chasing away the shadows,
so that she felt for that time immeasurably happy
and unsuspicious. She sat down at the laden
table, smiling again at the marvels which it
carried.

'My word, what a feast!' she said helplessly.
'Talk about the Ritz!'

Keith busied himself with the dishes. The
softly glowing cabin threw over Jenny its spell;
the comfort, the faint slow rocking of the yacht,
the sense of enclosed solitude, lulled her. Every
small detail of ease, which might have made her
nervous, merged with the others in a marvellous
contentment because she was with Keith, cut off
from the world, happy and at peace. If she
sighed, it was because her heart was full. But
she had forgotten the rest of the evening, her
shabbiness, every care that troubled her normal
days. She had cast these things off for the time,
and was in a glow of pleasure. She smiled at
Keith with a sudden mischievousness. They both
smiled, without guilt, and without guile, like two
children at a reconciliation.

VI

'Soup?' said Keith, and laid before her a steaming plate. 'All done by kindness.'

'Have you been cooking?' Some impulse made Jenny motherly. It seemed a strange reversal of the true order that he should cook for her. 'It's like *The White Cat* to have it. . . .'

'It's a secret,' Keith laughed. 'Tell you later. Fire away!' He tasted the soup, while Jenny looked at five little letter biscuits in her own plate. She spelt them out E T K I H—KEITH. He watched her, enjoying the spectacle of the naïve mind in action as the light darted into her face. 'I've got JENNY,' he said, embarrassed. She craned, and read the letters with open eyes of marvel. They both beamed afresh at the primitive fancy.

'How did you do it?' Jenny asked inquisitively. 'But it's nice.' They supped the soup. Followed, whitebait: thousands of little fish. . . . Jenny hardly liked to crunch them. Keith whipped away the plates, and dived back into the cabin with a huge pie that made her gasp. 'My gracious!' said Jenny. 'I can never eat it!'

'Not *all* of it,' Keith admitted. 'Just a bit, eh?' He carved.

'Oh, thank goodness it's not stew and bread and butter pudding!' cried Jenny, as the first mouthful of the pie made her shut her eyes tightly. 'It's like heaven!'

'If they have pies there.' Jenny had not meant that: she had meant only that her sensations were those of supreme contentment. 'Give me the old earth; and supper with Jenny!'

'Really?' Jenny was all brimming with delight.

'What will you have to drink? Claret? Burgundy?' Keith was again upon his feet. He poured out a large glass of red wine and laid it before her. Jenny saw with marvel the reflections of light on the wine and of the wine upon the tablecloth. She took a timid sip, and the wine ran tingling into her being.

'High life,' she murmured. 'Don't make me tipsy!' They exchanged overjoyed and intimate glances, laughing.

There followed trifle. Trifle had always been Jenny's dream; and this trifle was her dream come true. It melted in the mouth; its flavours were those of innumerable spices. She was transported with happiness at the mere thought of such trifle. As her palate vainly tried to unravel the secrets of the dish, Keith, who was closely observant, saw that she was lost in a kind of fanatical adoration of trifle.

'You like it?' he asked.

'I shall never forget it!' cried Jenny. 'Never as long as I live. When I'm an old . . . great-aunt . . .' She had hesitated at her destiny. 'I shall bore all the kids with tales about it. I shall say, "That night on the yacht . . . when I first

knew what trifle meant. . . ." They won't half
get sick of it. But I shan't.'

'You'll like to think about it?' asked Keith.
'Like to remember to-night?'

'Will *you*?' parried Jenny. 'The night you had
Jenny Blanchard to supper?' Their eyes met, in
a long and searching glance, in which candour
was not unmixed with a kind of measuring distrust.

VII

KEITH's face might have been carven for all the
truth that Jenny got from it then. There darted
across her mind the chauffeur's certainty that
she was to be his passenger. She took another
sip of wine.

'Yes,' she said again, very slowly. 'You *were*
sure I was coming. You got it all ready. Been
a bit of a sell if I hadn't come. You'd have had
to set to and eat it yourself. . . . Or get somebody
else to help you.'

She meant 'another girl,' but she did not know
she meant that until the words were spoken. Her
own meaning stabbed her heart. That icy knowledge that Keith was sure of her was bitterest of
all. It made her happiness defiant rather than
secure. He was the only man for her. How did
she know there were no other women for Keith?
How could she ever know that? Rather, it sank
into her consciousness that there must be other
women. His very ease showed her that. The

equanimity of his laughing expression brought her the unwelcome knowledge.

'I should have looked pretty small if I'd made no preparations, shouldn't I?' Keith inquired in a dry voice. 'If you'd come here and found the place cold and nothing to eat you'd have made a bit of a shindy.'

A reserve had fallen between them. Jenny knew she had been unwise. It pressed down upon her heart the feeling that he was somehow still a stranger to her. And all the time they had been apart he had not seemed a stranger, but one to whom her most fleeting and intimate thoughts might freely have been given. That had been the wonderful thought to her—that they had met so seldom and understood each other so well. She had made a thousand speeches to him in her dreams. Together, in these same dreams, they had seen and done innumerable things together, always in perfect confidence, in perfect understanding. Yet now, when she saw him afresh, all was different. Keith was different. He was browner, thinner, less warm in manner; and more familiar, too, as though he were sure of her. His clothes were different, and his carriage. He was not the same man. It was still Keith, still the man Jenny loved; but as though he were also somebody else whom she was meeting for the first time. Her love, the love intensified by long broodings, was as strong; but he was a stranger. All that intimacy which seemed to have been established between them once and for ever was broken by the new contact in unfamiliar surroundings. She was shy, uncertain, hesitating; and in her shyness she had blundered. She had been unwise, and he was offended when she could least afford to have him so offended. It took much resolution upon Jenny's part to essay the recovery of lost ground. But the tension was the worse for this mistake, and she suffered the more because of her anxious emotions.

'Oh, well,' she said at last, as calmly as she could, 'I daresay we should have managed. I mightn't have come. But I've come, and you had all these beautiful things ready; and . . .' Her courage to be severe abruptly failed; and lamely she concluded: 'And it's simply like fairyland. . . . I'm ever so happy.'

Keith grinned again, showing perfect white teeth. For a moment he looked, Jenny thought, quite eager. Or was that only her fancy because she so desired to see it? She shook her head; and that drew Keith's eye.

'More trifle?' he suggested, with an arch glance. Jenny noticed he wore a gold ring upon the little finger of his right hand. It gleamed in the faint glow of the cabin. So, also, did the fascinating golden hairs upon the back of his hand. Gently the cabin rose and fell, rocking so slowly that she could only occasionally be sure that the movement was true. She shook her head in reply.

'I've had one solid meal to-night,' she explained. 'Wish I hadn't! If I'd known I was coming out I'd have starved myself all day. Then you'd have been shocked at me!'

Keith demurely answered, as if to reassure her: 'Takes a lot to shock me. Have a peach?'

'I must!' she breathed. 'I can't let the chance slip. O-oh, what a scent!' She reached the peach towards him. 'Grand, isn't it!' Jenny discovered for Keith's quizzical gaze an unexpected dimple in each pale cheek. He might have been Adam, and she the original temptress.

'Shall I peel it?'

'Seems a shame to take it off!' Jenny watched his deft fingers as he stripped the peach. The glowing skin of the fruit fell in lifeless peelings upon his plate, dying as it were under her eyes. Keith had poured wine for her in another, smaller, glass. She shook her head.

'I shall be drunk!' she protested. 'Then I should sing! Horrible, it would be!'

'Not with a little port . . . I'm not pressing you to a lot. Am I?' He brought coffee to the table, and she began to admire first of all the pattern of the silver tray. Jenny had never seen such a tray before, outside a shop, nor so delicately porcelain a coffee-service. It helped to give her the sense of strange unforgettable experience.

'You didn't say if you'd remember this evening,' she slowly reflected. Keith looked sharply up from the coffee, which he was pouring, she saw, from a thermos flask.

'Didn't I?' he said. 'Of course I shall remember it. I've done better. I've looked forward to it. That's something you've not done. I've looked forward to it for weeks. You don't think of that. We've been in the Mediterranean, coasting about. I've been planning what I'd do when we got back. Then Templecombe said he'd be coming right up to London; and I planned to see you.'

'Templecombe?' Jenny queried. 'Who's he?'

'He's the lord who owns this yacht. Did you think it was my yacht?'

'No . . . I hoped it wasn't . . .' Jenny said slowly.

VIII

KEITH's eyes were upon her; but she looked at her peach stone, her hand still lightly holding the fruit knife, and her fingers half caught by the beam of a candle which stood beside her. He persisted:

'Well, Templecombe took his valet, who does the cooking; and my hand—my sailorman—wanted to go and visit his wife . . . and that left me to see after the yacht. D'you see? I had the choice of keeping Tomkins aboard, or staying aboard myself.'

'You might almost have given me longer notice,' urged Jenny. 'It seems to me.'

'No. I'm under instructions. I'm not a free man,' said Keith soberly. 'I was once; but I'm not now. I'm the captain of a yacht. I do what I'm told.'

Jenny fingered her port-wine glass, and in looking at the light upon the wine her eyes became fixed.

'Will you ever do anything else?' she asked. Keith shrugged slightly.

'You want to know a lot,' he said.

'I don't know very much, do I?' Jenny answered, in a little dead voice. 'Just somewhere about nothing at all. I have to pretend the rest.'

'D'you want to know it?'

Jenny gave a quick look at his hands which lay upon the table. She could not raise her eyes further. She was afraid to do so. Her heart seemed to be beating in her throat.

'It's funny me having to ask for it, isn't it!' she said, suddenly haggard.

VII. *MORTALS*

I

KEITH did not answer. That was the one certainty she had; and her heart sank. He did not answer. That meant that really she was nothing to him, that he neither wanted nor trusted her. And yet she had thought a moment before—only a moment before—that he was as moved as herself. They had seemed to be upon the brink of confidences; and now he had drawn back. Each instant deepened her sense of failure. When Jenny stealthily looked sideways, Keith sat staring before him, his expression unchanged. She had failed.

'You don't trust me,' she said, with her voice trembling. There was another silence. Then:

'Don't I?' Keith asked, indifferently. He reached his hand out and patted hers, even holding it lightly for an instant. 'I think I do. You don't think so?'

'No.' She merely framed the word, sighing.

'You're wrong, Jenny.' Keith's voice changed. He deliberately looked round the table at the little dishes that still lay there untouched. 'Have some of these sweets, will you. . . . No?' Jenny could only draw her breath sharply, shaking her head. 'Almonds, then?' She moved impatiently, her face distorted with wretched exasperation. As if he could see that, and as if fear of the outcome hampered his resolution, Keith hurried on. 'Well, look here: we'll clear the table together, if you like. Take the things through the other cabin—*that* one—to the galley; root up the table by its old legs—I'll show you how it's done;— and then we can have a talk. I'll . . . I'll tell you as much as I can about everything you want to know. That do?'

'I can't stay long. I've left Pa in bed.' She could not keep the note of roughness from her pleading voice, although shame at being petulant was struggling with her deeper feeling.

'Well, he won't want to get up again yet, will he?' Keith answered composedly. Oh, he had nerves of steel! thought Jenny. 'I mean, this *is* his bedtime, I suppose?' There was no answer. Jenny looked at the tablecloth, numbed by her sensations. 'Do you have to look after him all the time? That's a bit rough. . . .'

'No,' was forced from Jenny. 'No, I don't . . . not generally. But to-night—but that's a long story, too. With rows in it.' Which made Keith laugh. He laughed not quite naturally, forcing the last several jerks of his laughter, so that she shuddered at the thought of his possible con- tempt. It was as if everything she said was lost before ever it reached his heart—as if the words were like weak blows against an overwhelming strength. Discouragement followed and deepened after every blow—every useless and baffled word. There was again silence, while Jenny set her teeth, forcing back her bitterness and her chagrin, trying to behave as usual, and to check the throbbing within her breast. He was trying to charm her, teasingly to wheedle her back into kindness, altogether misunderstanding her mood. He was guarded and considerate when she wanted only passionate and abject abandonment of disguise.

'We'll toss up who shall begin first,' Keith said in a jocular way. 'How's that for an idea?'

Jenny felt her lips tremble. Frantically she shook her head, compressing the unruly lips. Only by keeping in the same position, by making herself remain still, could she keep back the tears. Her thought went on, that Keith was cruelly playing with her, mercilessly watching the effect of his own coldness upon her too sensitive heart. Eh, but it was a lesson to her! What brutes men could be, at this game! And that thought gave her, presently, an unnatural composure. If he were cruel, she would never show her wounds. She would sooner die. But her eyes, invisible to him, were dark with reproach, and her face drawn with agony.

'Well, we'd better do *something*,' she said, in a sharp voice; and rose to her feet. 'Where is it the things go?' Keith also rose, and Jenny felt suddenly sick and faint at the relaxation of her self-control.

II

'Hullo, hullo!' Keith cried, and was at once by her side. 'Here; have a drink of water.' Jenny, steadying herself by the table, sipped a little of the water.

'Is it the wine that's made me stupid?' she asked. 'I feel as if my teeth were swollen, and my skin was too tight for my bones. Beastly!'

'How horrid!' Keith said lightly, taking from her hand the glass of water. 'If it's the wine you won't feel the effects long. Go on deck if you like. You'll feel all right in the air. I'll clear away.' Jenny would not leave him. She shook her head decidedly. 'Wait a minute, then. I'll come too!'

They moved quickly about, leaving the fruit and little sweets and almonds upon the side-table, but carrying everything else through a sleeping-cabin into the galley. It was this other cabin that still further deepened Jenny's sense of pain—of inferiority. That was the feeling now most painful. She had just realised it. She was a common girl; and Keith—ah, Keith was secure enough, she thought.

In that moment Jenny deliberately gave him up. She felt it was impossible that he should love her. When she looked around it was with a sorrowfulness as of farewell. These things were the things that Keith knew and had known—that she would never again see but in the bitter memories of this night. The night would pass, but her sadness would remain. She would think of him here. She gave him up, quite humble in her perception of the disparity between them.

And yet her own love would stay, and she must store her memory full of all that she would want to know when she thought of his every moment. Jenny ceased to desire him. She somehow—it may have been by mere exhausted cessation of feeling—wished only to understand his life and then never to see him again. It was a kind of numbness that seized her. Then she awoke once again, stirred by the bright light and by the luxury of her surroundings.

'This where you sleep?' With passionate interest in everything that concerned him, Jenny looked eagerly about the cabin. She now indicated a broad bunk, with a beautifully white counterpane and such an eiderdown quilt as she might optimistically have dreamed about. The tiny cabin was so compact, and so marvellously furnished with beautiful things that it seemed to Jenny a kind of suite in tabloid form. She did not understand how she had done without all these luxurious necessities for five-and-twenty years.

'Sometimes,' Keith answered, having followed her marvelling eye from beauty to beauty. 'When there's company I sleep forward with the others.' He had been hurrying by with a cruet and the bread dish when her exclamation checked him.

'Is this lord a friend of yours, then?' Jenny asked.

'Sometimes,' Keith dryly answered. 'Understand?' Jenny frowned again at his tone.

'No,' she said. Keith passed on.

Jenny stood surveying the sleeping-cabin. A whole nest of drawers attracted her eye, deep drawers that would hold innumerable things. Then she saw a hand-basin with taps for hot and cold water. Impulsively she tried the hot-water tap, and was both relieved and disappointed when it gasped and offered her cold water. There were monogramed toilet appointments beautiful to see; a leather-cased carriage clock, a shelf full of books that looked fascinating; towels; tiny rugs; a light above the hand-basin, and another to switch on above the bunk. . . . It was wonderful! And there was a looking-glass before her in which she could see her own reflection as clear as day—too clearly for her pleasure!

The face she irresistibly saw in this genuine mirror looked pale and tired, although upon each white cheek there was a hard scarlet flush. Her eyes were liquid, the pupils dilated; her whole appearance was one of suppressed excitement. She had chagrin, not only because she felt that her appearance was unattractive, but because it seemed to her that her face kept no secrets. Had she seen it as that of another, Jenny would unerringly have read its painful message.

'Eh, dear,' she said aloud. 'You give yourself away, old sport! Don't you, now!' The mirrored head shook in disparaging admission of its own shortcoming. Jenny bent nearer, meeting the eyes with a clear stare. There were wretched

lines about her mouth. For the first time in her
life she had a horrified fear of growing older. It
was as though, when she shut her eyes, she saw
herself as an old woman. She felt a curious stab
at her heart.

Keith, returning, found Jenny still before the
mirror, engaged in this unsparing scrutiny; and,
laughing, gently, he caught her elbow with his
fingers. In the mirror their glances met. At his
touch Jenny thrilled, and unconsciously leaned
towards him. From the mirrored glance she
turned questioningly, to meet upon his face a
beaming expression of tranquil enjoyment that
stimulated her to candid remark. Somehow it
restored some of her lost ease to be able to
speak so.

'I look funny, don't I?' She appealed to his
judgment. Keith bent nearer, as for more detailed examination, retaining hold upon her
elbow. His face was tantalisingly close to hers,
and Jenny involuntarily turned her head away,
not coquettishly, but through embarrassment at
a mingling of desire and timidity.

'Is that the word?' he asked. 'You look all
right, my dear.'

My dear! She knew that the words meant
more to her than they did to him, so carelessly
were they uttered; but they sent a shock through
her. How Jenny wished that she might indeed
be dear to Keith! He released her, and she followed him, laden, backwards and forwards until

the table was cleared. Then he unscrewed the table legs, and the whole thing came gently away in his hands. There appeared four small brass sockets imbedded in the carpet's deep pile; and the centre of the room was clear. By the same dexterous use of his acquaintance with the cabin's mechanism, Keith unfastened one of the settees, and wheeled it forward so that it stood under the light, and in great comfort for the time when they should sit to hear his story.

'Now!' he said. 'We'll have a breather on deck to clear your old head.'

III

By this time the moon was silvering the river, riding high above the earth, serenely a thing of eternal mystery to her beholders. With the passing of clouds and the deepening of the night, those stars not eclipsed by the moon shone like swarmed throbbing points of silver. They seemed more remote, as though the clearer air had driven them farther off. Jenny, her own face and throat illumined, stared up at the moon, marvelling; and then she turned, without speaking, to the black shadows and the gliding, silent water. Upon every hand was the chequer of contrast, beautiful to the eye, and haunting to the spirit. A soft wind stirred her hair and made her bare her teeth in pleasure at the sweet contact.

Keith led her to the wide wooden seat which ran by the side of the deck, and they sat together

there. The noise of the city was dimmer; the
lamps were yellowed in the moon's whiter light;
there were occasional movements upon the face
of the river. A long way away they heard a sharp
panting as a motor boat rushed through the
water, sending a great surging wave that made
all other craft rise and fall and sway as the river's
agitation subsided. The boat came nearer, a
coloured light showing; and presently it hastened
past, a moving thing with a muffled figure at its
helm; and the *Minerva* rocked gently almost
until the sound of the motor boat's tuff-tuff had
been lost in the general noise of London. Nearer
at hand, above them, Jenny could hear the
clanging of tram-gongs and the clatter and slow
boom of motor omnibuses; but these sounds
were mellowed by the evening, and although
they were near enough to be comforting they
were too far away to interrupt this pleasant
solitude with Keith. The two of them sat in the
shadow, and Jenny craned to hear the chuckle
of the water against the yacht's sides. It was a
beautiful moment in her life. . . . She gave a little
moan, and swayed against Keith, her delight
succeeded by deadly languor.

IV

So for a moment they sat, Keith's arm around
her shoulders; and then Jenny moved so as to
free herself. She was restless and unhappy
again, her nerves on edge. The moon and the

water, which had soothed her, were now an irritation. Keith heard her breath come and go, quickly, heavily.

'Sorry, Jenny,' he said, in a tone of puzzled apology. She caught his fallen hand, pressing it eagerly.

'It's nothing. Only that minute. Like somebody walking on my grave.'

'You're cold. We'll go down to the cabin again.' He was again cool and unembarrassed. Together they stood upon the deck in the moonlight, while the water flowed rapidly beneath them and the night's mystery emphasised their remoteness from the rest of the world. They had no part, at this moment, in the general life; but were solitary, living only to themselves. . . .

Keith's arm was about her as they descended; but he let it drop as they stood once more in the golden-brown cabin. 'Sit here!' He plumped a cushion for her, and Jenny sank into an enveloping softness that rose about her as water might have done, so that she might have been alarmed if Keith had not been there looking down with such an expression of concern.

'I'm really all right,' she told him, reassuringly. 'Miserable for a tick—that's all!'

'Sure?' He seemed genuinely alarmed, scanning her face. She had again turned sick and faint, so that her knees were without strength. Was he sincere? If only she could have been sure of him. It meant everything in the world to her. If only Keith would say he loved her: if only he would kiss her! He had never done that. The few short days of their earlier comradeship had been full of delight; he had taken her arm, he had even had her in his arms during a wild bluster of wind; but always the inevitable kiss had been delayed, had been averted; and only her eager afterthoughts had made romance of their meagre acquaintance. Yet now, when they were alone, together, when every nerve in her body seemed tense with desire for him, he was somehow aloof—not constrained (for then she would have been happy, at the profoundly affecting knowledge that she had carried the day), but unsympathetically and unlovingly at ease. She could not read his face: in his manner she read only a barren kindness that took all and gave nothing. If he didn't love her she need not have come. It would have been better to go on as she had been doing, dreaming of him until—until what? Jenny sighed at the grey vision. Only hunger had driven her to his side on this evening —the imperative hunger of her nature upon which Keith had counted. He had been sure she would come—that was unforgivable. He had welcomed her as he might have welcomed a man; but as he might also have welcomed any man or woman who would have relieved his loneliness upon the yacht. Not a loved friend. Jenny, with her brain restored by the gentle breeze to its normal quickness of action, seemed

dartingly to seek in every direction for reassur-
ance; and she found in everything no single tone
or touch to feed her insatiable greed for tokens
of his love. Oh, but she was miserable indeed—
disappointed in her dearest and most secret
aspirations. He was perhaps afraid that she
wanted to attach herself to him? If that were so,
why couldn't he be honest, and tell her so? That
was all she wanted from him. She wanted only
the truth. She felt she could bear anything but
this kindness, this charming detached thought
for her. He was giving her courtesy when all she
needed was that his passion should approach her
own. And when she should have been strong,
mistress of herself, she was weak as water. Her
strength was turned, her self-confidence mocked
by his bearing. She trembled with the recurring vehemence of her love, that had been fed
upon solitude, upon the dreariness in which she
spent her mere calendared days. Her eyes were
sombrely glowing, dark with pain; and Keith
was leaning towards her as he might have leant
towards any girl who was half fainting. She
could have cried, but that she was too proud to
cry. She was not Emmy, who cried. She was
Jenny Blanchard, who had come upon this fool's
trip because a force stronger than her pride had
bidden her to forsake all but the impulse of her
love. And Keith, secure and confident, was
coolly, as it were, disentangling himself from the
claim she had upon him by virtue of her love. It

seemed to Jenny that he was holding her at a distance. Nothing could have hurt her more. It shamed her to think that Keith might suspect her honesty and her unselfishness. When she had thought of nothing but her love and the possibility of his own.

She read now, in this moment of descent into misery, a dreadful blunder made by her own overweening eagerness. She saw Keith, alone, thinking that he would be at a loss to fill his time, suddenly remembering her, thinking in a rather contemptuous way of their days together, and supposing that she would do as well as another for an hour's talk to keep him from a stagnant evening. If that were so, good-bye to her dreams. If she were no more to him than that there was no hope left in her life. For Keith might ply from port to port, seeing in her only one girl for his amusement; but he had spoilt her for another man. No other man could escape the withering comparison with Keith. To Jenny he was a king among men, incomparable; and if he did not love her, then the proud Jenny Blanchard who unhesitatingly saw life and character with an immovable reserve was the merest trivial legend of Kennington Park. She was like every other girl, secure in her complacent belief that she could win love—until the years crept by, and no love came, and she must eagerly seek to accept whatever travesty of love sidled within the radius of her attractiveness.

Suddenly Jenny looked at Keith.

'Better now,' she said harshly. 'You'll have to buck up with your tale—won't you! If you're going to get it out before I have to toddle home again.'

'Oh,' said Keith, in a confident tone. 'You're here now. You'll stay until I've quite finished.'

'What do you mean?' asked Jenny sharply. 'Don't talk rubbish!'

Keith held up a warning forefinger. He stretched his legs and drew from his pocket a stout pipe.

'I mean what I say.' He looked sideways at her. 'Don't be a fool, Jenny.'

Her heart was chilled at the menace of his words no less than by the hardness of his voice.

v

'I DON'T know what you're talking about, Keith; but you'll take me back to the steps when I say,' she said. Keith filled his pipe. 'I suppose you think it's funny to talk like that.' Jenny looked straight in front of her, and her heart was fluttering. It was not her first tremor; but she was deeply agitated. Keith, with a look that was almost a smile, finished loading the pipe and struck a match. He then settled himself comfortably at her side.

'Don't be a juggins, Jenny,' he remarked, in a dispassionate way that made her feel helpless.

'Sorry,' she said quickly. 'I've got the jumps.

I've had awful rows to-night . . . before coming out.'

'Tell me about them,' Keith urged. 'Get 'em off your chest.' She shook her head. Oh no, she wanted something from him very different from such kindly sympathy.

'Only makes it worse,' she claimed. 'Drives it in more. Besides, I don't want to. I want to hear about you.'

'Oh, me!' He made a laughing noise. 'There's nothing to tell.'

'You said you would.' Jenny was alarmed at his perverseness; but they were not estranged now.

Keith was smiling rather bitterly at his own thoughts, it seemed.

'I wonder why it is women want to know such a lot,' he said, drowsily.

'All of them?' she sharply countered. 'I suppose you ought to know.'

'You look seedy still. . . . Are you really feeling better?' Jenny took no notice. 'Well, yes; I suppose all of them. They all want to take possession of you. They're never satisfied with what they've got.'

'Perhaps they haven't got anything,' Jenny said. And after a painful pause: 'Oh, well: I shall have to be going home.' She wearily moved, in absolute despair, perhaps even with the notion of rising, though her mind was in turmoil.

'Jenny!' He held her wrist, preventing any

further movement. He was looking at her with an urgent gaze. Then, violently, with a rapid motion, he came nearer, and forced his arm behind Jenny's waist, drawing her close against his breast, her face averted until their cheeks touched, when the life seemed to go out of Jenny's body and she moved her head quickly in resting it on his shoulder, Keith's face against her hair, and their two hearts beating thickly. It was done in a second, and they sat so, closely embraced, without speech. Still Jenny's hands were free, as if they had been lifeless. Time seemed to stand still, and every noise to stop, during that long moment. And in her heart Jenny was saying over and over, utterly hopeless, 'It's no good; it's no good; it's no good. . . .' Wretchedly she attempted to press herself free, her elbow against Keith's breast. She could not get away; but each flying instant deepened her sense of bitter failure.

'It's no use,' she said at last, in a dreadful murmur. 'You don't want me a bit. Far better let me go.'

Keith loosed his hold, and she sat away from him with a little sigh that was almost a shudder. Her hands went as if by instinct to her hair, smoothing it. Another instinct, perhaps, made her turn to him with the ghost of a reassuring smile.

'Silly, we've been,' she said, huskily. 'I've been thinking about you all this time; and this is the end of it. Well, I was a fool to come. . . .'

She sat up straight, away from the back of the settee; but she did not look at Keith. She was looking at nothing. Only in her mind was going on the tumult of merciless self-judgment. Suddenly her composure gave way and she was again in his arms, not crying, but straining him to her. And Keith was kissing her, blessed kisses upon her soft lips, as if he truly loved her as she had all this time hoped. She clung to him in a stupor.

VIII. *PENALTIES*

I

'POOR old Jenny,' Keith was saying, stroking her arm and holding his cheek against hers.

'You don't want me . . .' groaned Jenny.

'Yes.'

'I can tell you don't. You don't mean it. D'you think I can't tell!'

Keith raised a finger and lightly touched her hair. He rubbed her cheek with his own, so that she could feel the soft bristles of his shaven beard. And he held her more closely within the circle of his arm.

'Because I'm clumsy?' he breathed. 'You know too much, Jenny.'

'No: I can tell. . . . It's all the difference in the world.'

'Well, then; how many others have kissed you? . . . Eh?'

'Keith!' Jenny struggled a little. 'Let me go now.'

'How many?' Keith kissed her cheek. 'Tell the whole dreadful truth.'

'If I asked you how many girls . . . what would you say then?' Jenny's sombre eyes were steadily watching him, prying into the secrets of his own. He gave a flashing smile, that lighted up his brown face.

'We're both jealous,' he told her. 'Isn't that what's the matter?'

'You don't trust me. You don't want me. You're only teasing.' With a vehement effort she recovered some of her self-control. Pride was again active, the dominant emotion. 'So am I only teasing,' she concluded. 'You're too jolly pleased with yourself.'

'How did you know I was clumsy?' Keith asked. 'I shall bite your old face. I shall nibble it . . . as if I was a horse . . . and you were a bit of sugar. Fancy Jenny going home with half a face!' He laughed excitedly at his forced pleasantry, and the sound of his laugh was music to Jenny's ears. He was excited. He was moved. Quickly the melancholy pressed back upon her after this momentary surcease. He was excited because she was in his arms—not because he loved her.

'Why did you send for me?' she suddenly said. 'In your letter you said you'd explain everything. Then you said you'd tell me about yourself. You've done nothing but tease all the time. . . . Are you afraid, or what? Keith, dear: you don't know what it means to me. If you don't want me—let me go. I oughtn't to have come. I was silly to come; but I had to. But if you only wanted somebody to tease . . . one of the others would have done quite as well.'

Again the smile spread across Keith's face, brightening his eyes and making his teeth glisten.

'I said you were jealous,' he murmured in her ear. 'One of the others, indeed! Jenny, there's no other—nobody like you, my sweet. There couldn't be. Do you think there could be?'

'Nobody such a fool,' Jenny said, miserably.

'Who's a fool? You?' He seemed to think for a moment; and then went on: 'Well, I've told you I planned the supper. . . . That was true.'

'Let me go. I'm getting cramped.' Jenny drew away; but he followed, holding her less vigorously, but in no way releasing her. 'No: really let me go.' Keith shook his head.

'I shan't let you go,' he said. 'Make yourself comfortable.'

'I only make myself miserable.' Jenny felt her hair, which was loosened. Her cheeks were hot.

'Are you sorry you came?'

'Yes.' Keith pressed closer to her, stifling her breath. She saw his brown cheeks for an instant before she was again enveloped in his strong embrace; and then she heard a single word breathed in her ear.

'Liar!' said Keith. In a moment he added: 'Sorry be pole-axed.'

II

IT was the second time in that evening that Jenny had been accused of lying; and when the charge had been brought by Alf she had flamed with anger. Now, however, she felt no anger. She felt through her unhappiness a dim motion

of exulting joy. Half suffocated, she was yet
thrilled with delight in Keith's strength, with
belief in his love because it was ardently shown.
Strength was her god. She worshipped strength
as nearly all women worship it. And to Jenny
strength, determination, manhood, were Keith's
attributes. She loved him for being strong; she
found in her own weakness the triumph of powerlessness, of humiliation.

'You're suffocating me,' she warned him,
panting.

'D'you love me a little?'

'Yes. A little.'

'A lot? Say you love me a lot! And you're
glad you came . . .'

Jenny held his face to hers, and kissed him
passionately.

'Dear!' she fiercely whispered.

Keith slowly released her, and they both
laughed breathlessly, with brimming, glowing
eyes. He took her hand, still smiling and watching her face.

'Old silly,' Keith murmured. 'Aren't you an
old silly! Eh?'

'So you say. You ought to know. . . . I suppose
I am . . .'

'But a nice old silly . . . And a good old girl to
come to-night.'

'But then you *knew* I should come,' urged
Jenny, drily, frowningly regarding him.

'You can't forgive that, can you! You think

I ought to have come grovelling to you. It's not proper to ask you to come to me . . . to believe you might come . . . to have everything ready in *case* you might come. Prude, Jenny! That's what you are.'

'A prude wouldn't have come.'

'That's all you know,' said Keith, teasingly. 'She'd have come—out of curiosity; but she'd have made a fuss. That's what prudes are. That's what they do.'

'Well, I expect you know,' Jenny admitted, sarcastically. The words wounded her more than they wounded him. Where Keith laughed, Jenny quivered. 'You don't know what it means to me——' she began again, and checked her too unguarded tongue.

'To come?' He bent towards her. 'Of course, it's marvellous to me! Was that what you meant?'

'No. To think . . . other girls . . .' She could not speak distinctly.

'Other girls?' Keith appeared astonished. 'Do you really believe . . .' He too paused. 'No other girls come on this yacht to see me. I've known other girls. I've made love to other girls—what man hasn't? You don't get to my age without...'

'Without what?' Jenny asked coolly.

'I'm not pretending anything to you. I'm thirty and a bit over. A man doesn't get to my age . . . No man does, without having been made a fool of.'

'Oh, I don't mind that,' Jenny said sharply. 'It's the girls you've fooled.'

'Don't you believe it, Jenny. They've always been wiser than me. Say they've known a bit more. You're different . . .' Jenny shook her head, sighing.

'I bet they've all been that,' she slowly said. 'Till the next one.' The old unhappiness had returned, gripping her heart. She no longer looked at him, but stared away, straight in front of her.

'Well, what if they had all been different?' Keith persisted. 'Supposing I were to tell you about them. Each one . . . There's no time for it, Jenny. You'll have to take my word for it. You'll do that if you want to. If you want to believe in me. Do you?'

'Of course I do!' Jenny blazed. 'I can't! Be different if I was at home. But I'm here, and you knew I'd come. D'you see what I mean?'

'You're not in a trap, old girl,' said Keith. 'You can go home this minute if you think you are.' His colour also rose. 'You make too much fuss. You want me to tell you good fat lies to save your face. Don't be a juggins, Jenny! Show your spirit! Jenny!'

Keith still held her hand. He drew it towards him, and Jenny was made to lean by his sudden movement. He slipped his arm again round her. Jenny did not yield herself. He was conscious of rebuff, although she did not struggle.

'You want me to trust you blindfold,' she said in a dreary voice. 'It's not good enough, Keith. Really it isn't! When you don't trust me. You sent for me, and I came. As soon as I was here you . . . you were as beastly as you could be . . .' Her voice trembled.

'Not really beastly . . .' Keith urged, and his coaxing tone and concerned expression shook her. 'Nice beastly, eh?'

'You weren't nice. You weren't . . .' Jenny hesitated. 'You didn't . . . you weren't nice.'

'I didn't want to frighten you.'

Jenny drew herself up, frantically angry.

'*Now* who's lying!' she savagely cried, and put her hands to disengage herself. 'Oh Keith, I'm so sick of it!' He held her more tightly. All her efforts were unavailing against that slowly increased pressure from his strong arms.

'Listen, Jenny,' Keith said. 'I love you. That's that. I wanted to see you more than anything on earth. I wanted to kiss you. Good God, Jen. . . . D'you think you're the easiest person in the world to manage?'

III

THE bewilderment that succeeded clove the silence. Jenny gasped against her will.

'What do you mean?' she demanded.

'You think I'm looking on you as cheap . . . when I'm in an absolute funk of you!' Keith cried.

'O-oh!' Her exclamation was incredulity itself. Keith persisted warmly:

'I'm not lying. It's all true. And you're a termagant, Jenny. That's what you are. You want it all your own way! Anything that goes wrong is my fault—not yours! You don't think there's anything that's your fault. It's all mine. But, my good girl, that's ridiculous. What d'you think I know about *you*? Eh? Nothing whatever! Absolutely nothing! You think you're as clear as day! You're not. You're a dark horse. I'm afraid of you—afraid of your temper . . . your pride. You won't see that. You think it's my fault that . . .' Keith's excitement almost convinced Jenny.

'Shouting won't do any good,' she said, deeply curious and overwhelmed by her bewilderment.

'Pull yourself together, Jenny!' he urged. 'Look at it from my side if you can. Try! Imagine I've got a side, that is. And now I'll tell you something about myself . . . no lies; and you'll have to make the best of the truth. The Truth!' Laughing, he kissed her; and Jenny, puzzled but intrigued, withheld her indignation in order to listen to the promised account. Keith began. 'Well, Jenny: I told you I was thirty. I'm thirty-one in a couple of months. I'll tell you the date, and you can work me a sampler. And I was born in a place you've never set eyes on—and I hope you never will set eyes on it. I was born in Glasgow. And there's a smelly old river there,

called the Clyde, where they launch big ships . . .
a bit bigger than the *Minerva*. The *Minerva* was
built in Holland. Well, my old father was a
tough old chap—not a Scotchman, though my
mother was Scotch—with a big business in Glasgow. He was as rich as—well, richer than anybody you ever met. Work that out! And he was
as tough as a Glasgow business man. They're
a special kind. And I was his little boy. He had
no other little boys. You interested?'

Jenny nodded sharply, her breast against his,
so that she felt every breath he drew.

'Yes: well, my father was so keen that I should
grow up into a Glasgow business man that he
nearly killed me. He hated me. Simply because
when I did anything it was always something
away from the pattern—the plan. D'you see?
And he'd nearly beat my head in each time. . . .
Yes, wasn't it! . . . Well, when I was ten he and
I had got into such a way that we were sworn
enemies. He'd got a strong will; but so had I,
even though I was such a kid. And I wouldn't—
I couldn't—do what he told me to. And when I
was thirteen, I ran away. I'd always loved the
river, and boats, and so on; and I ran away from
my old father. And he nearly went off his head
. . . and he brought me back. Didn't take him
long to find me! That was when I began to hate
him. I'd only been afraid of him before; but I
was growing up. Well, he put me to a school
where they watched me all the time. I sulked,

I worked, I did every blessed thing; and I grew older still, and more afraid of my father, and somehow less afraid of him, too. I got a sort of horror of him. I hated him. And when he said I'd got to go into the business I just told him I'd see him damned first. That was when he first saw that you can't make any man a slave—not even your own son—as long as he's got enough to eat. He couldn't starve me. It's starved men who are made slaves, Jenny. They've got no guts. Well, he threw me over. He thought I should starve myself and then go back to him, fawning. I didn't go. I was eighteen, and I went on a ship. I had two years of it; and my father died. I got nothing. All went to a cousin. I was nobody; but I was free. Freedom's the only thing that's worth while in this life. And I was twenty or so. It was then that I picked up a girl in London and tried to keep her—not honest, but straight to me. I looked after her for a year, working down by the river. But it was no good. She went off with other men because I got tired of her. I threw her over when I found that out. I mean, I told her she could stick to me or let me go. She wanted both. I went to sea again. It was then I met Templecombe. I met him in South America, and we got very pally. Then I came back to England. I got engaged to a girl— got married to her when I was twenty-three . . .'

'Married!' cried Jenny, pulling herself away. She had flushed deeply. Her heart was like lead.

'I'm not lying. You're hearing it all. And she's dead.'

'What was her name?'

'Adela. . . . She was little and fair; and she was a little sport. But I only married her because I was curious. I didn't care for her. In a couple of months I knew I'd made a mistake. She told me herself. She knew much more than I did. She was older than I was; and she knew a lot for her age—about men. She'd been engaged to one and another since she was fifteen; and in ten years you get to know a good deal. I think she knew everything about men—and I was a boy. She died two years ago. Well, after I'd been with her for a year I broke away. She only wanted me to fetch and carry. . . . She "took possession" of me, as they say. I went into partnership with a man who let me in badly; and Adela went back to her work and I went back to sea. And a year later I went to prison because a woman I was living with was a jealous cat and got the blame thrown on me for something I knew nothing about. D'you see? Prison. Never mind the details. When I came out of prison I was going downhill as fast as a barrel; and then I saw an advertisement of Templecombe's for a skipper. I saw him, and told him all about myself; and he agreed to overlook my little time in prison if I signed on with him to look after this yacht. Now you see I haven't got a very good record. I've been in prison; and I've lived with three women; and I've got no prospects except that I'm a good sailor and know my job. But I never did what I was sent to prison for; and, as I told you, the three women all knew more than I did. I've never done a girl any harm intentionally; and the last of them belongs to six years ago. Since then I've met other girls, and some of them have run after me because I was a sailor-man. They do, you know. You're the girl I love; and I want you to remember that I was a kid when I got married. That's the tale, Jenny; and every word of it's true. And now what d'you think of it? Are you afraid of me now? Don't you think I'm a bit of a fool? Or d'you think I'm the sort of fellow that fools the girls?'

There was no reply to his question for a long time; until Keith urged her afresh.

'What I'm wondering,' said Jenny, in a slow and rather puzzled way, 'is, what you'd think of me if I'd lived with three different men. Because I'm twenty-five, you know.'

IV

IT might have checked Keith in mid-career. His tone had certainly not been one of apology. But along with a natural complacency he had the honesty that sometimes accompanies success in affairs.

'Well,' he said frankly, 'I shouldn't like it, Jen.'

'How d'you think I like it?'

'D'you love me? Jenny, dear!'

'I don't know. I don't see why you should be different.'

'Nor do I. I am, though. I wish I wasn't. Can you see that? Have you ever wished you weren't yourself? Of course you have. So have I. Have you had men running after you all the time? Have you been free night and day, with time on your hands, and temptations going? You haven't. You don't know what it is. You've been at home. And what's more, you've been tied up because . . . because people think girls are safer if they're tied up.'

'*Men* do!' flashed Jenny. 'They like to have it all to themselves.'

'Well, if you'd ever been on your own for days together, and thinking as much about women as all young men do . . .'

'I wonder if I should boast of it,' Jenny said drily. 'To a girl I was pretending to love.'

Keith let his arm drop from her waist. He withdrew it, and sighed. Then he moved forward upon the settee, half rising, with his hands upon his knees.

'Ah well, Jenny: perhaps I'd better be taking you ashore,' he said in a constrained, exasperated tone.

'You don't care if you break my heart,' Jenny whispered. 'It's all one to you.'

'That's simply not true. . . . But it's no good discussing it.' He had lost his temper, and was full of impatience. He sat frowning, disliking her, with resentment and momentary aversion plainly to be seen in his bearing.

'Just because I don't agree that it's mighty kind of you to . . . condescend!' Jenny was choking. 'You thought I should jump for joy because other women had had you. I don't know what sort of girl you thought I was.'

'Well, I thought . . . I thought you were fond of me,' Keith slowly said, making an effort to speak coldly. 'That was what I thought.'

'Thought I'd stand anything!' she corrected. 'And fall on your neck into the bargain.'

'Jenny, old girl . . . That's not true. But I thought you'd understand better than you've done. I thought you'd understand *why* I told you. You think I thought I was so sure of you. . . . I wish you'd try to see a bit further.' He leaned back again, not touching her, but dejectedly frowning; his face pale beneath the tan. His anger had passed in a deeper feeling. 'I told you because you wanted to know about me. If I'd been the sort of chap you're thinking I should have told a long George Washington yarn, pretending to be an innocent hero. Well, I didn't. I'm not an innocent hero. I'm a man who's knocked about for fifteen years. You've got the truth. Women don't like the truth. They want a yarn. A yappy long sugar-coated yarn, and lots of protestations. This is all because I haven't asked you to forgive me—because I haven't

sworn not to do it again if only you'll forgive me.
You want to see yourself forgiving me. On a
pinnacle. .·. . Graciously forgiving me——'

'Oh, you're a beast!' cried Jenny. 'Let me go
home.' She rose to her feet, and stood in deep
thought. For a moment Keith remained seated;
then he too rose. They did not look at one
another, but with bent heads continued to re-
consider all that had been said.

V

'I've all the time been trying to show you I'm
not a beast,' Keith urged at last. 'But a human
being. It takes a woman to be something above
a human being.' He was sneering, and the sneer
chilled her.

'If you'd been thinking of somebody for
months,' she began in a trembling tone. 'Thinking about them all the time, living on it day after
day . . . just thinking about them and loving
them with all your heart. . . . You don't know
the way a woman does it. There's nothing else
for them to think about. I've been thinking
every minute of the day—about how you looked,
and what you said; and telling myself—though
I didn't believe it—that you were thinking about
me just the same. And I've been planning how
you'd look when I saw you again, and what we'd
say and do. . . . You don't know what it's meant
to me. You've never dreamed of it. And now to
come to-night—when I ought to be at home

looking after my dad. And to hear you talk about
... about a lot of other girls as if I was to take
them for granted. Why, how do I know there
haven't been lots of others since you saw me?'

'Because I tell you it's not so,' he interposed.
'Because I've been thinking of you all the time.'

'How many days at the seaside was it? Three?'

'It was enough for me. It was enough for you.'

'And now one evening's enough for both of
us,' Jenny cried sharply. 'Too much!'

'You'll cry your eyes out to-morrow,' he
warned.

'Oh, to-night!' she assured him recklessly.

'Because you don't love me. You throw all
the blame on me; but it's your own pride that's
the real trouble, Jenny. You want to come
round gradually; and time's too short for it.
Remember, I'm away again to-morrow. Did
you forget that?'

Jenny shivered. She had forgotten everything
but her grievance.

'How long will you be away?' she asked.

'Three months at least. Does it matter?' She
reproached his bitterness by a glance. 'Jenny
dear,' he went on; 'when time's so short, is it
worth while to quarrel? You see what it is: if
you don't try and love me you'll go home unhappy, and we shall both be unhappy. I told
you I'm not a free man. I'm not. I want to be
free. I want to be free all the time; and I'm
tied...'

'You're still talking about yourself,' said Jenny, scornfully, on the verge of tears.

VI

WELL, they had both made their unwilling attempts at reconciliation; and they were still further estranged. They were not loving one another; they were just quarrelsome and unhappy at being able to find no safe road of compromise. Jenny had received a bitter shock; Keith, with the sense that she was judging him harshly, was sullen with his deeply wounded heart. They both felt bruised and wretched, and deeply ashamed and offended. And then they looked at each other, and Jenny gave a smothered sob. It was all that was needed; for Keith was beside her in an instant, holding her unyielding body but murmuring gentle coaxing words into her ear. In an instant more Jenny was crying in real earnest, buried against him; and her tears were tears of relief as much as of pain.

IX. *WHAT FOLLOWED*

I

THE *Minerva* slowly and gently rocked with the motion of the current. The stars grew brighter. The sounds diminished. Upon the face of the river lights continued to twinkle, catching and mottling the wavelets. The cold air played with the water and flickered upon the *Minerva's* deck; strong enough only to appear mischievous, too soft and wayward to make its presence known to those within. And in the *Minerva's* cabin, set as it were in that softly rayed room of old gold and golden brown, Jenny was clinging to Keith, snatching once again at precarious happiness. Far off, in her aspirations, love was desired as synonymous with peace and contentment; but in her heart Jenny had no such pretence. She knew that it was otherwise. She knew that passive domestic enjoyment would not bring her nature peace, and that such was not the love she needed. Keith alone could give her true love. And she was in Keith's arms, puzzled and lethargic with something that was only not despair because she could not fathom her own feelings.

'Keith,' she said, presently. 'I'm sorry to be a fool.'

'You're *not* a fool, old dear,' he assured her. 'But I'm a beast.'

'Yes, I think you are,' Jenny acknowledged. There was a long pause. She tried to wipe her eyes, and at last permitted Keith to do that for her, flinching at contact with the handkerchief, but aware all the time of some secret joy. When she could speak more calmly she went on: 'Suppose we don't talk any more about being . . . what we are . . . and forgiving, and all that. We don't mean it. We only say it . . .'

'Well, I mean it—about being a beast,' Keith said humbly. 'That's because I made you cry.'

'Well,' said Jenny, agreeingly, 'you can be a beast—I mean, think you are one. And if I'm miserable I shall think I've been a fool. But we'll cut out about forgiving. Because I shall never really forgive you. I couldn't. It'll always be there, till I'm an old woman——'

'Only till you're happy, dear,' Keith told her. 'That's all that means.'

'I can't think like that. I feel it's in my bones. But you're going away. Where are you going? D'you know? Is it far?'

'We're going back to the South. Otherwise it's too cold for yachting. And Templecombe wants to keep out of England at the moment. He's safe on the yacht. He can't be got at. There's some wretched predatory woman of title pursuing him. . . .'

'Here . . . here!' cried Jenny. 'I can't understand if you talk pidgin-English, Keith.'

'Well . . . you know what ravenous means?

Hungry. And a woman of title—you know what a lord is. . . . Well, and she's chasing about, dropping little scented notes at every street corner for him.'

'Oh they are *awful*!' cried Jenny. 'Countesses! Always in the divorce court, or something. Somebody ought to stop them. They don't have countesses in America, do they? Why don't we have a republic, and get rid of them all? If they'd got the floor to scrub they wouldn't have time to do anything wrong.'

'True,' said Keith. 'True. D'you like scrubbing floors?'

'No. But I do it. And keep my hands nice, too.' The hands were inspected and approved.

'But then you're more free than most people,' Keith presently remarked, in a tone of envy.

'Free!' exclaimed Jenny. 'Me! In the millinery! When I've got to be there every morning at nine sharp or get the sack, and often, busy times, stick at it till eight or later, for a few bob a week. And never have any time to myself except when I'm tired out! Who gets the fun? Why, it's *all* work, for people like me; all work for somebody else. What d'you call being free? Aren't they free?'

'Not one. They're all tied up. Templecombe's hawk couldn't come on this yacht without a troop of friends. They can't go anywhere they like unless it's "the thing" to be done. They do everything because it's the right thing—because if they do something else people will think it's odd—think they're odd. And they can't stand that!'

'Well, but Keith! Who is it that's free?'

'Nobody,' he said.

'I thought perhaps it was only poor people . . . just *because* they were poor.'

'Well, Jenny. . . . That's so. But when people needn't do what they're told they invent a system that turns them into slaves. They have a religion or they run like the Gadarene swine into a fine old lather and pretend that everybody's got to do the same for some reason or other. They call it the herd instinct, and all sorts of names. But there's nobody who's really free. Most of them don't want to be. If they were free they wouldn't know what to do. If their chains were off they'd fall down and die. They wouldn't be happy if there wasn't a system grinding them as much like each other as it can.'

'But why not? What's the good of being alive at all if you've got to do everything whether you want to do it or not? It's not sense!'

'It's fact, though. From the king to the miner —all a part of a big complicated machine that's grinding us slowly to bits, making us all more and more wretched.'

'But who makes it like that, Keith?' cried Jenny. 'Who says it's to be so?'

Keith laughed grimly.

'Don't let's talk about it,' he urged. 'No good

talking about it. The only thing to do is to fight it—get out of the machine . . .'

'But there's nowhere to go, is there?' asked Jenny. 'I was thinking about it this evening. "They've" got every bit of the earth. Wherever you go "they're" there . . . with laws and police and things all ready for you. You've *got* to give in.'

'I'm not going to,' said Keith. 'I'll tell you that, Jenny.'

'But, Keith! Who is it that makes it so? There *must* be somebody to start it. Is it God?'

Keith laughed again, still more drily and grimly.

II

JENNY was not yet satisfied. She still continued to revolve the matter in her mind.

'You said nobody was free, Keith. But then you said you were free—when you got married.'

'*Till* I got married. Then I wasn't. I fell into the machine and got badly chawed then.'

'Don't you want to get married?' Jenny asked. 'Ever again?'

'Not that way.' Keith's jaw was set. 'I've been there; and to me that's what hell is.'

How Jenny wished she could understand! She did not want to get married herself—that way. But she wanted to serve. She wanted Keith to be her husband; she wanted to make him happy, and to make his home comfortable. She felt that to work for the man she loved was the way to be truly happy. Did he not think that he could be happy in working for her? She *couldn't* understand. It was all so hard that she sometimes felt that her brain was clamped with iron bolts and chains.

'What way d'you want to get married?' Jenny asked.

'I want to marry *you*. Any old way. And I want to take you to the other end of the world—where there aren't any laws and neighbours and rates and duties and politicians and imitations of life. . . . And I want to set you down on virgin soil and make a real life for you. In Labrador or Alaska . . .' He glowed with enthusiasm. Jenny glowed too, infected by his enthusiasm.

'Sounds fine!' she said. Keith exclaimed eagerly. He was alive with joy at her welcome.

'Would you come?' he cried. 'Really?'

'To the end of the world?' Jenny said. 'Rather!'

They kissed passionately, carried away by their excitement, brimming with joy at their agreement in feeling and desire. The cabin seemed to expand into the virgin forest and the open plain. A new vision of life was opened to Jenny. Exultingly she pictured the future, bright, active, occupied—away from the old cramping things. It was the life she had dreamed, away from men, away from stuffy rooms and endless millinery, away from regular hours and tedious meals, away from all that now made up her daily dullness. It was splendid! Her quick mind was at work, seeing, arranging, imagining as warm as life the changed days that would come in such a terrestrial Paradise. And then Keith, watching with triumph the mounting joy in her expression, saw the joy subside, the brilliance fade, the eagerness give place to doubt and then to dismay.

'What is it?' he begged. 'Jenny, dear!'

'It's Pa!' Jenny said. 'I couldn't leave him . . . not for anything!'

'Is that all? We'll take him with us!' cried Keith. Jenny sorrowfully shook her head.

'No. He's paralysed,' she explained, and sighed deeply at the faded vision.

III

'WELL, I'm not going to give up the idea for that,' Keith resumed, after a moment. Jenny shook her head, and a wry smile stole into her face, making it appear thinner than before.

'I didn't expect you would,' she said quietly. 'It's me that has to give it up.'

'Jenny!' He was astonished by her tone. 'D'you think I meant that? Never! We'll manage something. Something can be done. When I come back . . .'

'Ah, you're going away!' Jenny cried in agony. 'I shan't see you. I shall have every day to think of . . . day after day. And you won't write. And I shan't see you. . . .' She held him to her, her breast against his, desperate with the dread of being separated from him. 'It's easy for you, at sea, with the wind and the sun; and something fresh to see, and something happening all the time. But me—in a dark room, poring over bits of straw and velvet to make hats for soppy women, and then going home to old Em and stew for dinner. There's not much fun in it, Keith. . . . No, I didn't mean to worry you by grizzling. It's too bad of me! But seeing you, and hearing that plan, it's made me remember how beastly I felt before your letter came this evening. I was nearly mad with it. I'd been mad before; but never as bad as this was. And then your letter came—and I wanted to come to you; and I came, and we've wasted such a lot of time not understanding each other. Even now, I can't be sure you love me—not *sure*! I think you do; but you only say so. How's anyone ever to be sure, unless they know it in their bones? And I've been thinking about you every minute since we met. Because I never met anybody like you, or loved anybody before . . .'

She broke off, her voice trembling, her face against his, breathless and exhausted.

IV

'Now listen, Jenny,' said Keith. 'This is this. I love you, and you love me. That's right, isn't it? Well. I don't care about marriage—I mean, a ceremony; but you do. So we'll be married when

I come back in three months. That's all right,
isn't it? And when we're married, we'll either
take your father with us, what ever his health's
like; or we'll do something with him that'll do
as well. I should be ready to put him in somebody's care; but you wouldn't like that . . .'

'I love him,' Jenny said. 'I couldn't leave him
to somebody else for ever.'

'Yes. Well, you see there's nothing to be
miserable about. It's all straightforward now.
Nothing—except that we're going to be apart
for three months. Now, Jen: don't let's waste
any more time being miserable; but let's sit
down and be happy for a bit. . . . How's that?'

Jenny smiled, and allowed him to bring her
once again to the settee and to begin once more
to describe their future life.

'It's cold there, Jenny. Not warm at all.
Snow and ice. And you won't see anybody for
weeks and months—anybody but just me. And
we shall have to do everything for ourselves—
clothes, house-building, food catching and kill-
ing. . . . Trim your own hats. . . . Like the Swiss
Family Robinson; only you won't have everything growing outside as they did. And we'll go
out in canoes if we go on the water at all; and
see Indians—"Heap big man bacca" sort of
business—and perhaps hear wolves (I'm not
quite sure of that); and go about on sledges . . .
with dogs to draw them. But with all that we
shall be free. There won't be any bureaucrats to

tyrannise over us; no fashions, no regulations, no home-made laws to make dull boys of us. Just fancy, Jenny: nobody to *make* us do anything. Nothing but our own needs and wishes ...'

'I expect we shall tyrannise—as you call it—over each other,' Jenny said shrewdly. 'It seems to me that's what people do.'

'Little wretch!' cried Keith. 'To interrupt with such a thing. When I was just getting busy and eloquent. I tell you: there'll be inconveniences. You'll find you'll want somebody besides me to talk to and look after. But then perhaps you'll have somebody!'

'Who?' asked Jenny, unsuspiciously. 'Not Pa, I'm sure.'

Keith held her away from him, and looked into her eyes. Then he crushed her against him, laughing. It took Jenny quite a minute to understand what he meant.

'Very dull, aren't you!' cried Keith. 'Can't see beyond the end of your nose.'

'I shouldn't think it was hardly the sort of place for babies,' Jenny sighed. 'From what you say.'

v

KEITH roared with laughter, so that the *Minerva* seemed to shake in sympathy with his mirth.

'You're priceless!' he said. 'My bonny Jenny. I shouldn't think there was ever anybody like you in the world!'

'Lots of girls,' Jenny reluctantly suggested, shaking a dolorous head at the ghost of a faded vanity. 'I'm afraid.' She revived even as she spoke; and encouragingly added: 'Perhaps not exactly like.'

'I don't believe it! You're unique. The one and only Jenny Redington!'

'Red——!' Jenny's colour flamed. 'Sounds nice,' she said; and was then silent.

'When we're married,' went on Keith, watching her, 'where shall we go for our honeymoon? I say! . . . how would you like it if I borrowed the yacht from Templecombe and ran you off somewhere in it? I expect he'd let me have the old *Minerva*. Not a bad idea, eh what!'

'*When* we're married,' Jenny said breathlessly, very pale.

'What d'you mean?' Keith's eyes were so close to her own that she was forced to lower her lids. 'When I come back from this trip. Templecombe says three months. It may be less.'

'It may be more.' Jenny had hardly the will to murmur her warning—her distrust.

'Very unlikely; unless the weather's bad. I'm reckoning on a mild winter. If it's cold and stormy then of course yachting's out of the question. But we'll be back before the winter, any way. And then—darling Jenny—we'll be married as soon as I can get the licence. There's something for you to look forward to, my sweet. Will you like to look forward to it?'

Jenny could feel his breath upon her face; but she could not move or speak. Her breast was rising to quickened breathing; her eyes were burning; her mouth was dry. When she moistened her lips she seemed to hear a cracking in her mouth. It was as though fever were upon her, so moved was she by the expression in Keith's eyes. She was neither happy nor unhappy; but she was watching his face as if fascinated. She could feel his arm so gently about her shoulder, and his breast against hers; and she loved him with all her heart. She had at this time no thought of home; only the thought that they loved each other and that Keith would be away for three months; facing dangers indeed, but all the time loving her. She thought of the future, of that time when they both would be free, when they should no longer be checked and bounded by the fear of not having enough food. That was the thing, Jenny felt, that kept poor people in dread of the consequences of their own acts. And Jenny felt that if they might live apart from the busy world, enduring together whatever ills might come to them from their unsophisticated mode of life, they would be able to be happy. She thought that Keith would have no temptations that she did not share; no other men drawing him by imitativeness this way and that, out of the true order of his own character; no employer exacting in return for the weekly wage a servitude that was far from the blessed ideal of service.

Jenny thought these things very simply—impulsively—and not in a form to be intelligible if set down as they occurred to her; but the notions swam in her head along with her love for Keith and her joy in the love which he returned. She saw his dear face so close to her own, and heard her own heart thumping vehemently, quicker and quicker, so that it sounded thunderously in her ears. She could see Keith's eyes, so easily to be read, showing out the impulses that crossed and possessed his mind. Love for her she was sure she read, love and kindness for her, and mystification, and curiosity, and the hot slumbering desire for her that made his breathing short and heavy. In a dream she thought of these things, and in a dream she felt her own love for Keith rising and stifling her, so that she could not speak, but could only rest there in his arms, watching that beloved face and storing her memory with its precious betrayals.

Keith gently kissed her, and Jenny trembled. A thousand temptations were whirling in her mind—thoughts of his absence, their marriage, memory, her love. . . . With an effort she raised her lips again to his, kissing him in passion, so that when he as passionately responded it seemed as though she fainted in his arms and lost all consciousness but that of her love and confidence in him and the eager desire of her nature to yield itself where love was given.

X. CINDERELLA

I

THROUGH the darkness, and into the brightness of the moon's light, the rolling notes of Big Ben were echoing and re-echoing, as each stroke followed and drove away the lingering waves of its predecessor and was in turn dispersed by the one that came after. The sounds made the street noises sharper, a mere rattle against the richness of the striking clock. It was an hour that struck; and the quarters were followed by twelve single notes. Midnight. And Jenny Blanchard was still upon the *Minerva*; and Emmy and Alf had left the theatre; and Pa Blanchard was alone in the little house in Kennington Park.

The silvered blackness of the *Minerva* was disturbed. A long streak of yellow light showed from the door leading into the cabin while yet the sounds of the clock hung above the river. It became ghostly against the moonlight that bleached the deck, a long grey-yellow finger pointing the way to the yacht's side.

Jenny and Keith made their way up the steps and to the deck, and Jenny shivered a little in the strong light. Her face was in shadow. She hurried, restored to sanity by the sounds and the thought of her father. Horror and self-blame were active in her mind—not from the fear of discovery; but from shame at having for so long deserted him.

'Oh, hurry!' Jenny whispered, as Keith slipped over the side of the yacht into the waiting dinghy. There was a silence, and presently the heavy cludder of oars against the boat's side.

'Jenny! Come along!' called Keith from the water.

Not now did Jenny shrink from the running tide. Her one thought was to get home; and she had no inclination to think of what lay between her and Kennington Park. She hardly understood what Keith said as he rowed to the steps. She saw the bridge looming, its black shadow cutting the water that sparkled so dully in the moonlight; and then she saw the steps leading from the bridge to the river's edge. They were alongside; she was ashore; and Keith was pressing her hand in parting. Still she could not look at him until she was at the top of the steps, when she turned and raised her hand in farewell.

II

SHE knew she had to walk for a little way down the road in the direction of her home, and then up a side street, where she had been told that she would find the motor car awaiting her. And for some seconds she could not bear the idea of speaking to the chauffeur, from the sense that he must know exactly how long she had been on board the yacht. The hesitation caused her to linger, as the cold air had caused her to think. It was as though she feared that when he was found the man would be impudent to her, and leer, behaving familiarly as he might have done to a common woman. Because she was alone and unprotected. It was terrible. Her secret filled her with the sense of irremediable guilt. Already she was staled with the evening's excitement. She stopped and wavered, her shadow, so black and small, hesitating as she did. Could she walk home? She looked at the black houses, and listened to the terrifying sinister roar that continued faintly to fill the air. Could she go by tram? If she did—whatever she did—the man might wait for her all night, and Keith would know how cowardly she had been. It might even come to the ears of Lord Templecombe, and disgrace Keith before him. To go or to stay was equally to bring acute distress upon herself, the breathless shame of being thought disgraced for ever. Already it seemed to her that the shadows were peopled with observers ready to spy upon her, to seize her, to bear her away into hidden places. . . .

At last, her mind resolved by her fears, which crowded upon her in a tumult, Jenny stepped fearfully forward. The car was there, dimly outlined, a single light visible to her eye. It was drawn up at the side of the street; and the chauffeur was fast asleep, his head upon his arms, and his arms spread upon the steering-wheel.

'I say!' cried Jenny in a panic, glancing quickly over her shoulder at unseen dangers. 'Wake up! Wake up!'

She stepped into the car, and it began to quiver with life as the engine was started. Then, as if drowned in the now familiar scent of the hanging bouquet, Jenny lay back once more in the soft cushions; bound for home, for Emmy and Alf and Pa; her evening's excursion at an end, and only its sequel to endure.

Part Three

MORNING

XI. *AFTER THE THEATRE*

I

AFTER leaving the house Emmy and Alf pressed along in the darkness, Alf's arm still surrounding and supporting Emmy, Emmy still half jubilantly and half sorrowfully continuing to recognise her happiness and the smothered chagrin of her emotions. She was not able to feel either happy or miserable; but happiness was uppermost. Dislike of Jenny had its place, also; for she could account for every weakness of Alf's by reference to Jenny's baseness. But indeed Emmy could not think, and could only passively and excitedly endure the conflicting emotions of the moment. And Alf did not speak, but hurried her along as fast as his strong arm could secure her compliance with his own pace; and they walked through the night-ridden streets and full into the blaze of the theatre entrance without any words at all. Then, when the staring vehemence of the electric lights whitened and shadowed her face, Emmy drew away, casting down her eyes, alarmed at the disclosures which the brilliance might devastatingly make. She slipped from his arm, and stood rather forlornly while Alf fished in his pockets for the tickets. With docility she followed him, thrilled when he stepped aside in passing the commissionaire and took her arm. Together

they went up the stairs, the heavy carpets with
their drugget covers silencing every step, the
gilded mirrors throwing their reflections backwards and forwards until the stairs seemed
peopled with hosts of Emmys and Alfs. As they
drew near the closed doors of the circle the hush
filling the staircases and vestibules of the theatre
was intensified. An aproned attendant seemed
to Emmy's sensitiveness to look them up and
down and superciliously to disapprove them.
She moved with indignation. A dull murmur,
as of single voices, disturbed the air somewhere
behind the rustling attendant: and when the
doors were quickly opened Emmy saw beyond
the darkness and the intrusive flash of light caused
by the opening doors a square of brilliance and
a dashing figure upon the stage talking staccato.
Those of the audience who were sitting near the
doors turned angrily and with curiosity to view
the new-comers; and the voice that Emmy had
distinguished went more stridently on, with a
strong American accent. In a flurry she found
and crept into her seat, trying to understand the
play, to touch Alf, to remove her hat, to disci-
pline her excitements. And the staccato voice
went on and on, detailing a plan of some sort
which she could not understand because they
had missed the first five minutes of the play.
Emmy could not tell that the actor was only
pretending to be an American; she could not
understand why, having spoken twenty words,

he must take six paces farther from the foot-
lights until he had spoken thirteen more; but
she could and did feel most overwhelmingly
exuberant at being as it were alone in that
half-silent multitude, sitting beside Alf, their
arms touching, her head whirling, her heart
beating, and a wholly exquisite warmth flushing
her cheeks.

II

THE first interval found the play well advanced.
A robbery had been planned—for it was a 'crook'
play—and the heroine had already received wild-
eyed the advances of a fur-coated millionaire.
When the lights of the theatre popped up, and
members of the orchestra began once more un-
mercifully to tune their instruments, it was possible to look round at the not especially large
audience. But in whichever direction Emmy
looked she was always brought back as by a
magnet to Alf, who sat ruminantly beside her.
To Alf's sidelong eye Emmy was looking sur-
prisingly lovely. The tired air and the slightly
peevish mouth to which he was accustomed had
given place to the flush and sparkle of an excited
girl. Alf was aware of surprise. He blinked. He
saw the lines smoothed away from round her
mouth—the lines of weariness and dissatisfaction,
—and was tempted by the softness of her cheek.
As he looked quickly off again he thought how
full Jenny would have been of comment upon

the play, how he would have sat grinning with precious enjoyment at her merciless gibes during the whole of the interval. He had the sense of Jenny as all movement, as flashing and drawing him into quagmires of sensation, like a will-o'-the-wisp. Emmy was not like that. She sat tremulously smiling, humble before him, diffident, flattering. She was intelligent: that was it. Intelligent was the word. Not lively, but restful. Critically he regarded her. Rather a nice girl, Emmy. . . .

Alf roused himself, and looked around.

'Here, miss!' he called; and 'S-s-s-s' when she did not hear him. It was his way of summoning an attendant or a waitress. 'S-s-s-s.' The attendant brought chocolates, which Alf handed rather magnificently to his companion. He plunged into his pockets—in his rough-and-ready, muscular way—for the money, leaning far over the next seat, which was unoccupied. 'Like some lemon?' he said to Emmy. Together they inspected the box of chocolates, which contained much imitation-lace paper and a few sweets. 'Not half a sell,' grumbled Alf to himself, thinking of the shilling he had paid; but he looked with gratification at Emmy's face as she enjoyingly ate the chocolates. As her excitement a little strained her nervous endurance Emmy began to pale under the eyes; her eyes seemed to grow larger; she lost the first air of sparkle, but she became more pathetic. 'Poor little thing,' thought Alf, feeling masculine. 'Poor little thing: she's tired. Poor little thing.'

III

In the middle of this hot, excitedly-talking audience, they seemed to bask as in a warm pool of brilliant light. The brilliants in the dome of the theatre intensified all the shadows, heightened all the smiles, illumined all the silken blouses and silver bangles, the flashing eyes, the general air of fête.

'All right?' Alf inquired protectively. Emmy looked in gratitude towards him.

'Lovely,' she said. 'Have another?'

'I meant, *you*,' he persisted. 'Yourself, I mean.' Emmy smiled, so happily that nobody could have been unmoved at the knowledge of having given such pleasure.

'Oh, grand!' Emmy said. Then her eyes contracted. Memory came to her. The angry scene that had passed earlier returned to her mind, hurting her, and injuring her happiness. Alf hurried to engage her attention, to distract her from thoughts that had in them such discomfort as she so quickly showed.

'Like the play? I didn't quite follow what it was this old general had done to him. Did you?'

'Hadn't he kept him from marrying . . .' Emmy looked conscious for a moment. 'Marrying the right girl? I didn't understand it either. It's only a play.'

'Of course,' Alf agreed. 'See how that girl's eyes shone when old fur-coat went after her? Fair shone, they did. Like lamps. They'd got the limes on her. . . . You couldn't see them. My—er—my friend's the electrician here. He says it drives him nearly crazy, the way he has to follow her about in the third act. She . . . she's got some pluck, he says; the way she fights three of them single-handed. They've all got revolvers. She's got one; but it's not loaded. Lights a cigarette, too, with them all watching her, ready to rush at her.'

'There!' said Emmy, admiringly. She was thinking: 'It's only a play.'

'She gets hold of his fur coat, and puts it on. . . . Imitates his voice. . . . You can see it's her all the time, you know. So could they, if they looked a bit nearer. However, they don't. . . . I suppose there wouldn't be any play if they did. . . .'

Emmy was not listening to him: she was dreaming. She was gauche and simple in his company as a young girl would have been; but her mind was different. It was practical in its dreams, and they had their disturbing unhappiness, as well, from the greater poignancy of her desire. She was not a young girl, to be agreeably fluttered and to pass on to the next admirer without a qualm. She loved him, blindly but painfully; without the ease of young love, but with all the sickness of first love. And she had jealousy, the feeling that she was not his first object, to

poison her feelings. She could not think of Jenny
without tremors of anger. And still, for pain, her
thoughts went throbbing on about Jenny whenever, in happiness, she had seen a home and Alf
and a baby and the other plain clear consequences of earning his love—of taking him from
Jenny.

And then the curtain rose, the darkness fell,
and the orchestra's tune slithered into nothing.
The play went on, about the crook and the
general and the millionaire and the heroine and
all their curiously simple-minded friends. And
every moment something happened upon the
stage, from fights to thefts, from kisses (which
those in the gallery, not wholly absorbed by the
play, generously augmented) to telephone calls,
plots, speeches (many speeches, of irreproachable
moral tone), shoutings, and sudden wild appeals
to the delighted occupants of the gallery. And
Emmy sat through it hardly heeding the uncommon events, aware of them as she would
have been aware of distant shouting. Her attention was preoccupied with other matters. She
had her own thoughts, serious enough in themselves. Above all, she was enjoying the thought
that she was with Alf, and that their arms were
touching; and she was wondering if he knew that.

IV

THROUGH another interval they sat with silent
embarrassment, the irreplaceable chocolates,

which had earlier been consumed, having served their turn as a means of devouring attention. Alf was tempted to fly to the bar for a drink and composure, but he did not like to leave Emmy; and he could not think of anything which could safely be said to her in the middle of this gathering of hot and radiant persons. 'To speak' in such uproar meant 'to shout.' He felt that every word he uttered would go echoing in rolls and rolls of sound out among the multitude. They were not familiar enough to make that a matter of indifference to him. He was in the stage of secretiveness. And Emmy, after trying once or twice to open various small topics, had fallen back upon her own thoughts, and could invent nothing to talk about until the difficulties that lay between them had been removed. Her brow contracted. She moved her shoulders, or sat pressed reservedly against the back of her seat. Her voice, whenever she did not immediately hear some word fall from Alf, became sharp and self-conscious—almost 'managing.'

It was a relief to both of them, and in both the tension of sincere feeling had perceptibly slackened, when the ignored orchestra gave way before the rising curtain. Again the two drew together in the darkness, as all other couples were doing, comforted by proximity, and even by the unacknowledged mutual pleasure of it; again they watched the extraordinary happenings upon the stage. The fur coat was much used, cigarettes were lighted and flung away with prodigal recklessness, pistols were revealed—one of them was even fired into the air;—and jumping, trickling music heightened the effects of a number of strong speeches about love, and incorruptibility, and womanhood. . . . The climax was reached. In the middle of the climax, while yet the lover wooed and the villain died, the audience began to rustle, preparatory to going home. Even Emmy was influenced to the extent of discovering and beginning to adjust her hat. It was while she was pinning it, with her elbows raised, that the curtain fell. Both Emmy and Alf rose in the immediately successive re-illumination of the theatre; and Emmy looked so pretty with her arms up, and with the new hat so coquettishly askew upon her head, and with a long hatpin between her teeth, that Alf could not resist the impulse to put his arm affectionately round her in leading the way out.

V

AND then, once in the street, he made no scruple about taking Emmy's arm within the crook of his as they moved from the staring whiteness of the theatre lamps out into the calmer moonshine. It was eleven o'clock. The night was fine, and the moon rode high above amid the twinkling stars. When Alf looked at Emmy's face it was transfigured in this beautiful light, and he drew her gently from the direct way back to the little house.

'Don't let's go straight back,' he said. 'Stroll ull do us good.'

Very readily Emmy obeyed his guidance. Her heart was throbbing; but her brain was clear. He wanted to be with her; and the knowledge of that made Emmy happier than she had been since early childhood.

'It's been lovely,' she said, with real warmth of gratitude, looking away from him with shyness.

'Hm,' growled Alf, in a voice of some confusion. 'Er . . . you don't go much to the theatre, do you?'

'Not much,' Emmy agreed. 'See, there's Pa. He always looks to me . . .'

'Yes.' Alf could not add anything to that for a long time. 'Fine night,' he presently recorded. 'D'you like a walk! I mean . . . I'm very fond of it, a night like this. Mr. Blanchard's all right, I suppose?'

'Oh yes. *She's* there.' Emmy could not bring herself to name Jenny to him. Yet her mind was busy thinking of the earlier jar, recomposing the details, recalling the words that had passed. Memory brought tears into her eyes; but she would not allow Alf to see them, and soon she recovered her self-control. It had to be spoken of: the evening could not pass without reference to it; or it would spoil everything. Alf would think of her—he was bound to think of her—as a crying, petulant, jealous woman, to whom he had been merely kind. Patronising, even! Perhaps, even, the remembrance of it would prevent him from coming again to the house. Men like Alf were so funny in that respect. It took so little to displease them, to drive them away altogether. At last she ventured: 'It was nice of you to take me.'

Alf fidgeted, jerking his head, and looking recklessly about him.

'Not at all,' he grumbled. 'Not tired, are you?' Emmy reassured him. 'What I mean, I'm very glad. . . . Now, look here, Em. May as well have it out. . . .' Emmy's heart gave a bound: she walked mechanically beside him, her head as stiffly held as though the muscles of her neck had been paralysed. 'May as well, er . . . have it out,' repeated Alf. 'That's how I am—I like to be all shipshape from the start. When I came along this evening I *did* mean to ask young Jen to go with me. That was quite as you thought. I never thought you'd, you know, *care* to come with me. I don't know why; but there it is. I never meant to put it like I did . . . in that way . . . to have a fuss and upset anybody. I've . . . I mean, she's been out with me half a dozen times; and so I sort of naturally thought of her.'

'Of course,' agreed Emmy. 'Of course.'

'But I'm glad you came,' Alf said. Something in his honesty, and the brusqueness of his rejoicing, touched Emmy, and healed her first wound—the thought that she might have been unwelcome to him. They went on a little way, more at ease; both ready for the next step in intimacy which was bound to be taken by one of them.

'I thought she might have said something to you—about me not *wanting* to come,' Emmy proceeded, tentatively. 'Made you think I never wanted to go out.'

Alf shook his head. Emmy had there no opening for her resentment.

'No,' he said, with stubborn loyalty. 'She's always talked very nice about you.'

'What does she say?' swiftly demanded Emmy.

'I forget. . . . Saying you had a rough time at home. Saying it was rough on you. That you're one of the best . . .'

'*She* said that?' gasped Emmy. 'It's not like her to say that. Did she really? She's so touchy about me, generally. Sometimes, the way she goes on, anybody'd think I was the miserablest creature in the world, and always on at her about something. I'm not, you know; only she thinks it. Well, I can't help it, can I? If you knew how I have to work in that house, you'd be . . . surprised. I'm always at it. The way the dirt comes in—you'd wonder where it all came from! And see, there's Pa and all. She doesn't take that into account. She gets on all right with him; but she isn't there all day, like I am. That makes a difference, you know. He's used to me. She's more of a change for him.'

Alf was cordial in agreement. He was seeing

all the difference between the sisters. In his heart there still lingered a sort of cherished enjoyment of Jenny's greater spirit. Secretly it delighted him, like a forbidden joke. He felt that Jenny—for all that he must not, at this moment, mention her name—kept him on the alert all the time, so that he was ever in hazardous pursuit. There was something fascinating in such excitement as she caused him. He never knew what she would do or say next; and while that disturbed and distressed him it also lacerated his vanity and provoked his admiration. He admired Jenny more than he could ever admire Emmy. But he also saw Emmy as different from his old idea of her. He had seen her trembling defiance early in the evening, and that had moved him and made him a little afraid of her; he had also seen her flushed cheeks at the theatre, and Emmy had grown in his eyes suddenly younger. He could not have imagined her so cordial, so youthful, so interested in everything that met her gaze. Finally, he found her quieter, more amenable, more truly wifely than her sister. It was an important point in Alf's eyes. You had to take into account—if you were a man of common sense—relative circumstances. Devil was all very well in courtship; but mischief in a girl became contrariness in a domestic termagant. That was an idea that was very much in Alf's thoughts during this walk, and it lingered there like acquired wisdom.

'Say she's going with a sailor?' he suddenly demanded.

'So she told me. I've never seen him. She doesn't tell lies, though.'

'I thought you said she did!'

Emmy flinched: she had forgotten the words spoken in her wild anger, and would have been ashamed to account for them in a moment of greater coolness.

'I mean, if she says he's a sailor, that's true. She told me he was on a ship. I suppose she met him when she was away that time. She's been very funny ever since. Not funny—restless. Anything I've done for her she's made a fuss. I give her a thorough good meal; and oh! there's such a fuss about it. "Why don't we have ice creams, and merangs, and wine, and grouse, and sturgeon——"'

'Ph! Silly talk!' said Alf, in contemptuous wonder. 'I mean to say . . .'

'Oh, well: you know what flighty girls are. He's probably a swank-pot. A steward, or something of that sort. I expect he has what's left over, and talks big about it. But she's got ideas like that in her head, and she thinks she's too good for the likes of us. It's too much trouble to her to be pelite these days. I've got the fair sick of it, I tell you. And then she's always out. . . . *Somebody's* got to be at home, just to look after Pa and keep the fire in. But Jenny—oh dear no! She's no sooner home than she's out again.

Can't rest. Says it's stuffy indoors, and off she goes. I don't see her for hours. Well, I don't know . . . but if she doesn't quiet down a bit she'll only be making trouble for herself later on. She can't keep house, you know! She can scrub; but she can't cook so very well, or keep the place nice. She hasn't got the patience. You think she's doing the dusting; and you find her groaning about what she'd do if she was rich. "Yes," I tell her; "it's all very well to do that; but you'd far better be doing something *useful*," I say. "Instead of wasting your time on idle fancies."'

'Very sensible,' agreed Alf, completely absorbed in such a discourse.

'She's trying, you know. You can't leave her for a minute. She says I'm stodgy; but I say it's better to be practical than flighty. Don't you think so, Alf?'

'Exackly!' said Alf, in a tone of the gravest assent. 'Exackly.'

VI

'I MEAN,' pursued Emmy, 'you must have a *little* common sense. But she's been spoilt—she's the youngest. I'm a little older than she is . . . *wiser*, I say; but she won't have it. . . . And Pa's always made a fuss of her. Really, sometimes, you'd have thought she was a boy. Racing about! My word, such a commotion! And then going out to the millinery, and getting among a lot of other girls. You don't know *who* they are—if they're

ladies or not. It's not a good influence for
her . . .'

'She ought to get out of it,' Alf said. To
Emmy it was a ghastly moment.

'She'll never give it up,' she hurriedly said.
'You know, it's in her blood. Off she goes! And
they make a fuss of her. She mimics everybody,
and they laugh at it—they think it's funny to
mimic people who can't help themselves—if they
are a bit comic. So she goes; and when she does
come home Pa's so glad to see a fresh face that
he makes a fuss of her, too. And she stuffs him
up with all sorts of tales—things that never happened—to keep him quiet. She says it gives him
something to think about. . . . Well, I suppose it
does. I expect you think I'm very unkind to say
such things about my own sister; but really I
can't help seeing what's under my nose; and
I sometimes get so—you know, worked up, that
I don't know how to hold myself. She doesn't
understand what it is to be cooped up indoors all
day long, like I am; and it never occurs to her to
say "Go along, Em; you run out for a bit." I
have to say to her; "You be in for a bit, Jen?"
and then she p'tends she's always in. And then
there's a rumpus. . . .'

Alf was altogether subdued by this account: it
had that degree of intimacy which, when one is
in a sentimental mood, will always be absorbing.
He felt that he really was getting to the bottom
of the mystery known to him as Jenny Blanchard.

The picture had verisimilitude. He could see Jenny as he listened. He was seeing her with the close and searching eye of a sister, as nearly true, he thought, as any vision could be. Once the thought 'I expect there's another story' came sidling into his head; but it was quickly drowned in further reminiscence from Emmy, so that it was clearly a dying desire that he felt for Jenny. Had Jenny been there, to fling her gage into the field, Alf might gapingly have followed her, lost again in admiration of her more sparkling tongue and equipments. But in such circumstances the arraigned party is never present. If Jenny had been there the tale could not have been told. Emmy's virtuous and destructive monologue would not merely have been interrupted: it would have been impossible. Jenny would have done all the talking. The others, all amaze, would have listened with feelings appropriate to each, though with feelings in common unpleasant to be borne.

'I bet there's a rumpus,' Alf agreed. 'Old Jen's not one to take a blow. She ups and gets in the first one.' He couldn't help admiring Jenny, even yet. So he hastened to pretend that he did not admire her; out of a kind of tact. 'But of course . . . that's all very well for a bit of sport, but it gets a bit wearisome after a time. I know what you mean . . .'

'Don't think I've been complaining about her,' Emmy said. 'I wouldn't. Really, I wouldn't.

Only I do think sometimes it's not quite fair that she should have all the fun, and me none of it. I don't want a lot. My tastes are very simple. But when it comes to none at all—well, Alf, what do *you* think?'

'It's a bit thick,' admitted Alf. 'And that's a fact.'

'See, she's always having her own way. Does just what she likes. There's no holding her.'

'Wants a man to do that,' ruminated Alf, with a half chuckle. 'Eh?'

'Well,' said Emmy, a little brusquely, 'I pity the man who tries it on.'

VII

EMMY was not deliberately trying to secure from Alf a proposal of marriage. She was trying to show him the contrast between Jenny and herself, and to readjust the balances as he appeared to have been holding them. She wanted to impress him. She was as innocent of any other intention as any girl could have been. It was jealousy that spoke; not scheme. And she was perfectly sincere in her depreciation of Jenny. She could not understand what it was that made the admiring look come into the faces of those who spoke to Jenny, nor why the unwilling admiration that started into her own heart should ever find a place there. She was baffled by character, and she was engaged in the common task of rearranging life to suit her own temperament.

They had been walking for some little distance now along deserted streets, the moon shining upon them, their steps softly echoing, and Emmy's arm as warm as toast. It was like a real lovers' walk, she could not help thinking, half in the shadow and wholly in the stillness of the quiet streets. She felt very contented; and with her long account of Jenny already uttered, and her tough body already reanimated by the walk, Emmy was at leisure to let her mind wander among sweeter things. There was love, for example, to think about; and when she glanced sideways Alf's shoulder seemed such a little distance from her cheek. And his hand was lightly clasping her wrist. A strong hand, was Alf's, with a broad thumb and big capable fingers. She could see it in the moonlight, and she had suddenly an extraordinary longing to press her cheek against the back of Alf's hand. She did not want any silly nonsense, she told herself; and the tears came into her eyes, and her nose seemed pinched and tickling with the cold at the mere idea of any nonsense; but she could not help longing with the most intense longing to press her cheek against the back of Alf's hand. That was all. She wanted nothing more. But that desire thrilled her. She felt that if it might be granted she would be content, altogether happy. She wanted so little!

And as if Alf too had been thinking of somebody nearer to him than Jenny, he began:

'I don't know if you've ever thought at all about me, Em. But your saying what you've done . . . about yourself . . . it's made me think a bit. I'm all on my own now—have been for years; but the way I live isn't good for anyone. It's a fact it's not. I mean to say, my rooms that I've got . . . they're not big enough to swing a cat in; and the way the old girl at my place serves up the meals is a fair knock-out, if you notice things like I do. If I think of her, and then about the way you do things, it gives me the hump. Everything you do's so nice. But with her—the plates have still got bits of yesterday's mustard on them, and all fluffy from the dishcloth . . .'

'Not washed prop'ly,' Emmy interestedly remarked; 'that's what that is.'

'Exackly. And the meat's raw inside. Cooks it too quickly. And when I have a bloater for my breakfast—I'm partial to a bloater—it's black outside, as if it was done in the cinders; and then inside—well, I like them done all through, like any other man. Then I can't get her to get me gammon rashers. She will get these little tiddy rashers, with little white bones in them. Why, while you're cutting them out the bacon gets cold. You may think I'm fussy . . . fiddly with my food. I'm not, really; only I like it . . .'

'Of course you do,' Emmy said. 'She's not interested, that's what it is. She thinks anything's food; and some people don't mind at all what they eat. They don't notice.'

'No. I *do*. If you go to a restaurant you get it different. You get more of it, too. Well, what with one thing and another I've got very fed up with Madame Bucks. It's all dirty and half baked. There's great holes in the carpet of my sitting-room—holes you could put your foot through. And I've done that, as a matter of fact. Put my foot through and nearly gone over. *Should* have done, only for the table. Well, I mean to say . . . you can't help being fed up with it. But she knows where I work, and I know she's hard up; so I don't like to go anywhere else, because if anybody asked me if he should go there, I couldn't honestly recommend him to; and yet, you see how it is, I shouldn't like to leave her in the lurch, if she knew I was just gone somewhere else down the street.'

'No,' sympathetically agreed Emmy. 'I quite see. It's very awkward for you. Though it's no use being too kind-hearted with these people; because they *don't* appreciate it; and if you don't say anything they just go on in the same way, never troubling themselves about you. They think, as long as you don't say anything you're all right; and it's not their place to make any alteration. They're quite satisfied. Look at Jenny and me.'

'Is she satisfied?' asked Alf.

'With herself, she is. She's never satisfied with me. She never tries to see it from my point of view.'

'No,' Alf nodded his head wisely. 'That's what it is. They don't.' He nodded again.

'Isn't it a lovely night,' ventured Emmy. 'See the moon over there.'

They looked up at the moon and the stars and the unfathomable sky. It took them at once away from the streets and the subject of their talk. Both sighed as they stared upwards, lost in the beauty before them. And when at last their eyes dropped, the street lamps had become so yellow and tawdry that they were like stupid spangles in contrast with the stars. Alf still held Emmy's arm so snugly within his own, and her wrist was within the clasp of his fingers. It was so little a thing to slide his fingers into a firm clasp of her hand, and they drew closer.

'Lovely, eh!' Alf ejaculated, with a further upward lift of his eyes. Emmy sighed again.

'Not like down here,' she soberly said.

'No, it's different. Down here's all right, though,' Alf assured her. 'Don't you think it is?' He gave a rather nervous little half laugh. 'Don't you think it is?'

'Grand!' Emmy agreed, with the slightest hint of dryness.

'I say, it was awfully good of you to come to-night,' said Alf. 'I've . . . you've enjoyed it, haven't you?' He was looking sharply at her, and Emmy's face was illumined. He saw her soft cheeks, her thin soft little neck; he felt her warm gloved hand within his own. 'D'you mind?' he asked, and bent abruptly so that their faces were close together. For a moment, feeling so daring that his breath caught, Alf could not carry out his threat. Then, roughly, he pushed his face against hers, kissing her. Quickly he released Emmy's arm, so that his own might be more protectingly employed; and they stood embraced in the moonlight.

VIII

IT was only for a minute, for Emmy, with instinctive secrecy, drew away into the shadow. At first Alf did not understand, and thought himself repelled; but Emmy's hands were invitingly raised. The first delight was broken. One more sensitive might have found it hard to recapture; but Alf stepped quickly to her side in the shadow, and they kissed again. He was surprised at her passion. He had not expected it, and the flattery was welcome. He grinned a little in the safe darkness, consciously and even sheepishly, but with eagerness. They were both clumsy and a little trembling, not very practised lovers, but curious and excited. Emmy felt her hat knocked a little sideways upon her head.

It was Emmy who moved first, drawing herself away from him, she knew not why.

'Where you going?' asked Alf, detaining her. 'What is it? Too rough, am I?' He could not see Emmy's shaken head, and was for a moment puzzled at the ways of woman—so far from his grasp.

'No,' Emmy said. 'It's wonderful.'

Peering closely, Alf could see her eyes shining.

'D'you think you're fond enough of me, Emmy?' She demurred.

'That's a nice thing to say! As if it was for me to tell you!' she whispered archly back.

'What ought I to say? I'm not . . . mean to say, I don't know how to say things, Emmy. You'll have to put up with my rough ways. Give us a kiss, old sport.'

'How many more! You *are* a one!' Emmy was not pliant enough. In her voice there was the faintest touch of—something that was not self-consciousness, that was perhaps a sense of failure. Perhaps she was back again suddenly into her maturity, finding it somehow ridiculous to be kissed and to kiss with such abandon. Alf was not baffled, however. As she withdrew he advanced, so that his knuckle rubbed against the brick wall to which Emmy had retreated.

'I say,' he cried sharply. 'Here's the wall.'

'Hurt yourself?' Emmy quickly caught his hand and raised it, examining the knuckle. The skin might have been roughened; but no blood was drawn. Painfully, exultingly, her dream realised, she pressed her cheek against the back of his hand.

IX

'WHAT's that for?' demanded Alf.

'Nothing. Never you mind. I wanted to do it.' Emmy's cheeks were hot as she spoke; but Alf marvelled at the action, and at her confession of such an impulse.

'How long had you . . . wanted to do it?'

'Mind your own business. The idea! Don't you know better than that?' Emmy asked. It made him chuckle delightedly to have such a retort from her. And it stimulated his curiosity.

'I believe you're a bit fond of me,' he said. 'I don't see why. There's nothing about me to write home about, I shouldn't think. But there it is: love's a wonderful thing.'

'Is it?' asked Emmy, distantly. Why couldn't he say he loved her? Too proud, was he? Or was he shy? He had only used the word 'love' once, and that was in this general sense—as though there *was* such a thing. Emmy was shy of the word, too; but not as shy as that. She was for a moment anxious, because she wanted him to say the word, or some equivalent. If it was not said, she was dependent upon his charity later, and would cry sleeplessly at night for want of sureness of him.

'D'you love me?' she suddenly said. Alf whistled. He seemed for that instant to be quite taken aback by her inquiry. 'There's no harm in me asking, I suppose.' Into Emmy's voice there came a thread of roughness.

'No harm at all,' Alf politely said. 'Not at all.' He continued to hesitate.

'Well?' Emmy waited, still in his arms, her ears alert.

'We're engaged, aren't we?' Alf muttered shamefacedly. 'Erum . . . what sort of ring would you like? I don't say you'll get it . . . and it's too late to go and choose one to-night.'

Emmy flushed again: he felt her tremble.

'You *are* in a hurry,' she said, too much moved for her archness to take effect.

'Yes, I am.' Alf's quick answer was reassuring enough. Emmy's heart was eased. She drew him nearer with her arms about his neck, and they kissed again.

'I wish you'd say you love me,' she whispered. 'Mean such a lot to me.'

'No!' cried Alf incredulously. 'Really?'

'Do you?'

'I'll think about it. Do you—me?'

'Yes. I don't mind saying it if you will.'

Alf gave a little whistle to himself, half under his breath. He looked carefully to right and left, and up at the house-wall against which they were standing. Nobody seemed to be in danger of making him feel an abject fool by overhearing such a confession as he was invited to make; and yet it was such a terrible matter. He was confronted with a difficulty of difficulties. He looked at Emmy, and knew that she was waiting, entreating him with her shining eyes.

'Er,' said Alf, reluctantly and with misgiving. 'Er . . . well, I . . . a . . . suppose I do . . .'

Emmy gave a little cry, that was half a smothered laugh of happiness at her triumph. It was not bad! She had made him admit it on the first evening. Later, when she was more at ease, he should be more explicit.

X

'Well,' said Alf, instantly regretting his admission, and inclined to bluster. 'Now I suppose you're satisfied?'

'Awfully!' breathed Emmy. 'You're a dear good soul. You're splendid, Alf!'

For a few minutes more they remained in that benign, unforgettable shadow; and then, very slowly, with Alf's arm about Emmy's waist, and Emmy's shoulder so confidingly against his breast, they began to return homewards. Both spoke very subduedly, and tried to keep their shoes from too loudly striking the pavement as they walked; and the wandering wind came upon them in glee round every corner, and rustled like a busybody among all the consumptive bushes in the front gardens they passed. Sounds carried far. A long way away they heard the tramcars grinding along the main road. But here all was hush, and the beating of two hearts in unison; and to both of them happiness lay ahead. Their aims were similar, in no point jarring or divergent. Both wanted a home, and loving labour, and quiet evenings of pleasant occupation. To both the daily work came with regularity, not as an intrusion or a wrong to manhood and womanhood; it was inevitable, and was regarded as inevitable. Neither Emmy nor Alf ever wondered why they should be working hard when the sun shone and the day was fine. Neither compared the lot accorded by station with an ideal fortune of blessed ease. They were not temperamentally restless. They both thought, with a practical sense that is as convenient as it is generally accepted, 'somebody must do the work: may as well be me.' No discontent would be theirs. And Alf was a good worker at the bench, a sober and honest man; and Emmy could make a pound go as far as any other woman in Kennington Park. They had before them a faithful future of work in common, of ideals (workaday ideals) in common; and at this instant they were both marvellously content with the immediate outlook. Not for them to change the order of the world.

'I feel it's so suitable,' Emmy startingly said, in a hushed tone, as they walked. 'Your . . . you know . . . "supposing you do" . . . me; and me . . . doing the same for you.'

Alf looked solemnly round at her. His Emmy skittish? It was not what he had thought. Still, it diverted him; and he ambled in pursuit.

'Yes,' he darkly said. 'What do you "suppose you do" for me?'

'Why, love you,' Emmy hurried to explain, trapping herself by speed into the use of the tabooed word. 'Didn't you know? Though it seems funny to say it, like that. It's so new. I've never dared to . . . you know . . . say it. I mean, we're both of us quiet, and reliable . . . we're neither of us flighty, I mean. That's why I think we suit each other—better than if we'd been different. Not like we are.'

'I'm sure we do,' Alf said.

'Not like some people. You can't help wondering to yourself however they came to get married. They seem so unlike. Don't they. It's funny. Ah well, love's a wonderful thing—as you say!' She turned archly to him, encouragingly.

'You seem happy,' remarked Alf, in a critical tone. But he was not offended; only tingled into desire for her by the strange gleam of merriment crossing her natural seriousness, the jubilant note of happy consciousness that the evening's love-making had bred. Alf drew her more closely to his side, increasingly sure that he had done well. She was beginning to intrigue him. With an emotion that startled himself as much as it delighted Emmy, he said thickly in her ear, 'D'you love me . . . like this?'

XI

THEY neared the road in which the Blanchards lived: Emmy began to press forward as Alf

seemed inclined to loiter. In the neighbourhood
the church that had struck eight as they left the
house began once again to record an hour.

'By George!' cried Alf. 'Twelve. . . . Midnight!' They could feel the day pass.

They were at the corner, beside the little
chandler's shop which advertised to the moon
its varieties of tea; and Alf paused once again.

'Half a tick,' he said. 'No hurry, is there?'

'You'll come in for a bit of supper,' Emmy
urged. Then, plumbing his hesitation, she went
on, in a voice that had steel somewhere in its
depths. 'They'll both be gone to bed. She won't
be there.'

'Oh, I wasn't thinking of that,' Alf declared,
with unconvincing nonchalance.

'I'll give you a drop of Pa's beer,' Emmy said
drily.

She took out a key, and held it up for his in-
spection.

'I say!' Alf pretended to be surprised at the
sight of a key.

'Quite a big girl, aren't I! Well, you see:
there are two, and Pa never goes out. So we
have one each. Saves a lot of bother.' As she
spoke Emmy was unlocking the door and enter-
ing the house. 'See, you can have supper with
me, and then it won't seem so far to walk home.
And you can throw Madame Bucks's rinds at the
back of the fire. You'll like that; and so will she.'

Alf, now perfectly docile, and even thrilled

with pleasure at the idea of being with her for a little while longer, followed Emmy into the passage, where the flickering gas showed too feeble a light to be of any service to them. Between the two walls they felt their way into the house, and Alf softly closed the door.

'Hang your hat and coat on the stand,' whispered Emmy, and went tiptoeing forward to the kitchen. It was in darkness. 'Oo, she is a monkey! She's let the fire out,' Emmy continued, in the same whisper. 'Have you got a match? The gas is out.' She opened the kitchen door wide, and stood there taking off her hat, while Alf fumbled his way along the passage. 'Be quick,' she said.

Alf pretended not to be able to find the matches, so that he might give her a hearty kiss in the darkness. He was laughing to himself because he had only succeeded, in his random venture, in kissing her chin; and then, when she broke away with a smothered protest and a half laugh, he put his hand in his pocket again for the match-box. The first match fizzed along the box as it was struck, and immediately went out.

'Oh, *do* hurry up!' cried Emmy in a whisper, thinking he was still sporting with her. 'Don't keep on larking about, Alf!'

'I'm not!' indignantly answered the delinquent. 'It wouldn't strike. Half a tick!'

He moved forward in the darkness, to be nearer the gas; and as he took the step his foot caught against something upon the floor. He exclaimed.

'Now what is it?' demanded Emmy. For answer Alf struck his match, and they both looked at the floor by Alf's feet. Emmy gave a startled cry and dropped to her knees.

'Hul-lo!' said Alf; and with his lighted match raised he moved to the gas, stepping, as he did so, over the body of Pa Blanchard, which was lying at full length across the kitchen floor.

XII. *CONSEQUENCES*

I

IN the succeeding quietness, Emmy fumbled at the old man's hands; then quickly at his breast, near the heart. Trembling violently, she looked up at Alf as if beseeching his aid. He too knelt, and Emmy took Pa's lolling head into her lap, as though by her caress she thought to restore colour and life to the features. The two discoverers did not speak nor reason: they were wholly occupied with the moment's horror. At last Alf said, almost in a whisper:

'I think it's all right. He's hit his head. Feel his head, and see if it's bleeding.'

Emmy withdrew one hand. A finger was faintly smeared with blood. She shuddered, looking in horror at the colour against her hand; and Alf nodded sharply at seeing his supposition verified. His eye wandered from the insensible body, to a chair, to the open cupboard, to the topmost shelf of the cupboard. Emmy followed his glance point by point, and in conclusion they looked straight into each other's eyes, with perfect understanding. Alf's brows arched.

'Get some water—quick!' Emmy cried sharply. She drew her handkerchief from her breast as Alf returned with a jugful of water; and, having folded it, she dangled the kerchief in the jug.

'Slap it on!' urged Alf. 'He can't feel it, you know.'

So instructed, Emmy first of all turned Pa's head to discover the wound, and saw that her skirt was already slightly stained by the oozing blood. With her wetted handkerchief she gently wiped the blood from Pa's hair. It was still quite moist, and more blood flowed at the touch. That fact made her realise instinctively that the accident, the stages of which had been indicated by Alf's wandering glances, had happened within a short time previous to their return. Then, as Alf took the jug and threw some of its contents upon the old man's grey face, splashing her, she made an impatient gesture of protest.

'No, no!' she cried. 'It's all over *me*!'

'Been after his beer, he has,' Alf unnecessarily explained. 'That's what it is. Got up on the chair, and fell off it, trying to get at it. Bad boy!'

As she did not answer, from the irritation caused by nervous apprehensiveness, he soaked his own handkerchief and began to slap it across Pa's face, until the jug was empty. Alf thoughtfully sprinkled the last drops from it so that they fell cascading about Pa. He was turning away to refill the jug, when a notion occurred to him.

'Any brandy in the house?' he asked. 'Ought to have thought of it before. Pubs are all closed now.'

'See if there's any . . . up there.' Emmy pointed vaguely upwards. She was bent over Pa, gently wiping the trickles of water from his ghastly face, caressing with her wet handkerchief the closed eyes and the furrowed brow.

Alf climbed upon the chair from which Pa had fallen, and reached his hand round to the back of the high shelf, feeling for whatever was there. With her face upturned, Emmy watched and listened. She heard a very faint clink, as if two small bottles had been knocked together, and then a little dump, as if one of them had fallen over.

'Glory!' said Alf, still in the low voice that he had used earlier. 'Believe I've got it!'

'Got it? Is there any in it?' Emmy at the same instant was asking.

Alf was sniffing at the little bottle which he had withdrawn from the cupboard. He then descended carefully from the chair, and held the uncorked bottle under her nose, for a corroborative sniff. It was about half full of brandy. Satisfied, he knelt as before, now trying, however, to force Pa's teeth apart, and rubbing some of the brandy upon the parted lips.

'This'll do it!' Alf cheerfully and reassuringly cried. 'Half a tick. I'll get some water to wet his head again.' He stumbled once more out into the scullery, and the careful Emmy unconsciously flinched as she heard the jug struck hard in the darkness against the tap. Her eye was fixed upon the jug as it was borne brimming and splashing back to her side. She could not help feeling such housewifely anxiety even amid the tremors of her other acute concern. As Alf knelt he lavishly sprinkled some more water upon Pa's face, and set the jug ready to Emmy's hand, working with a quiet deftness that aroused her watchful admiration. He was here neither clumsy nor rough: if his methods were as primitive as the means at hand his gentle treatment of the senseless body showed him to be adaptable to an emergency. How she loved him! Pride gleamed in Emmy's eyes. She could see in him the eternal handy-man of her delight, made for husbandhood and as clearly without nonsense as any working wife could have wished.

Pa's nightshirt was blackened with great splashes of water, and the soaked parts clung tightly to his breast. At the neck it was already open, and they both thought they could see at this moment a quick contraction of the throat. An additional augury was found in the fact that Alf simultaneously had succeeded in dribbling some of the brandy between Pa's teeth, and although some of it ran out at the corners of his mouth and on to his cheeks, some also was retained and would help to revive him. Alf gave another quick nod, this time one of satisfaction.

'Feel his heart!' Emmy whispered. He did so. 'Can you feel it?'

'It's all right. Famous!'

Pa gave a little groan. He seemed to stir. Emmy felt his shoulders move against her knees; and she looked quickly up, a faint relieved smile crossing her anxious face. Then, as Alf returned her glance, his eyes became fixed, and he looked beyond her and up over her head. Jenny stood in the doorway, fully dressed, but without either hat or coat, her face blanched at the picture before her.

II

To Jenny, coming with every precautionary quietness into the house, the sight came as the greatest shock. She found the kitchen door ajar, heard voices, and then burst upon the three feebly illumined figures. Emmy, still in her out-of-doors coat, knelt beside Alf upon the floor; and between them, with a face terribly grey, lay Pa, still in his old red nightshirt, with one of his bare feet showing. The stained shirt, upon which the marks of water, looking in this light perfectly black, might have been those of blood, filled Jenny with horror. It was only when she saw both Emmy and Alf staring mutely at her that she struggled against the deadly faintness that was thickening a veil of darkness before her eyes. It was a dreadful moment.

'Hullo Jen!' Alf said. 'Look here!'

'I thought you must be in bed,' Emmy murmured. 'Isn't it awful!'

Not a suspicion! Her heart felt as if somebody

had sharply pinched it. They did not know she had been out! It made her tremble in a sudden flurry of excited relief. She quickly came forward, bending over Pa. Into his cheeks there had come the faintest wash of colour. His eyelids fluttered. Jenny stooped and took his hand, quite mechanically, pressing it between hers and against her heart. And at that moment Pa's eyes opened wide, and he stared up at her. With Alf at his side and Emmy behind him, supporting his head upon her lap, Pa could see only Jenny, and a twitching grin fled across his face—a grin of loving recognition. It was succeeded by another sign of recovery, a peculiar fumbling suggestion of remembered cunning.

'Jenny, my dearie,' whispered Pa, gaspingly. 'A good . . . boy!' His eyes closed again.

Emmy looked in quick challenge at Alf, as if to say, 'You see how it is! She comes in last, and it's her luck that he should see her. . . . *Always* the same!' And Jenny was saying, very low:

'It looks to me as if you'd been a bad boy!'

'Can't be with him *all* the time!' Emmy put in, having reached a point of general self-defence in the course of her mental explorations. She was recovering from her shock and her first horrible fears.

'Shall we get him to bed? Carry him back in there?' Jenny asked. 'The floor's soaking wet.' She had not to receive any rebuke: Emmy, although shaken, was reviving in happiness and in graciousness with each second's diminution of her dread. She now agreed to Pa's removal; and they all stumbled into his bedroom and laid him upon his own bed. Alf went quickly back again to the kitchen for the brandy; and presently a good dose of this was sending its thrilling and reviving fire through Pa's person. Emmy had busied herself in making a bandage for his wounded head; and Jenny had arranged him more comfortably, drying his chest and laying a little towel between his body and the night-shirt lest he should take cold. Pa was very complacently aware of these ministrations, and by the time they were in full order completed he was fast asleep, having expressed no sort of contrition for his naughtiness or for the alarm he had given them all.

Reassured, the party returned to the kitchen.

III

ALF could not wait to sit down to supper; but he drank a glass of beer, after getting it down for himself and rather humorously illustrating how Pa's designs must have been frustrated. He then, with a quick handshake with Jenny, hurried away.

'I'll let you out,' Emmy said. There were quick exchanged glances. Jenny was left alone in the kitchen for two or three minutes until Emmy returned, humming a little self-consciously, and no longer pale.

'Quite a commotion,' said Emmy, with assumed ease.

Jenny was looking at her, and Jenny's heart felt as though it were bursting. She had never in her life known such a sensation of guilt—guilt at the suppression of a vital fact. Yet above that sense of guilt, which throbbed within all her consciousness, was a more superficial concern with the happenings of the moment.

'Yes,' Jenny said. 'And . . . Had you been in long?' she asked quickly.

'Only a minute. We found him like that. We didn't come straight home.'

'Oh,' said Jenny, significantly, though her heart was thudding. 'You didn't come straight home.' Emmy's colour rose still higher. She faltered slightly, and tears appeared in her eyes. She could not explain. Some return of her jealousy, some feeling of what Jenny would 'think,' checked her. The communication must be made by other means than words. The two sisters eyed each other. They were very near, and Emmy's lids were the first to fall. Jenny stepped forward, and put a protective arm round her; and as if Emmy had been waiting for that she began smiling and crying at one and the same moment.

'Looks to me as if . . . ' Jenny went on after this exchange.

'I'm sorry I was a beast,' Emmy said. 'I'm as different as anything now.'

'You're a dear!' Jenny assured her. 'Never mind about what you said.'

It was an expansive moment. Their hearts were charged. To both the evening had been the one poignant moment of their lives, an evening to provide reflections for a thousand other evenings. And Emmy was happy, for the first time for many days, with the thought of happy life before her. She described in detail the events of the theatre and the walk. She did not give an exactly true story. It was not to be expected that she would do so. Jenny did not expect it. She gave indications of her happiness, which was her main object; and she gave further indications, less intentional, of her character, as no author can avoid doing. And Jenny, immediately discounting, and in the light of her own temperament re-shaping and re-proportioning the form of Emmy's narrative, was like the eternal critic—apprehending only what she could personally recognise. But both took pleasure in the tale, and both saw forward into the future a very satisfactory ending to Emmy's romance.

'And we got back just as twelve was striking,' Emmy concluded.

A deep flush overspread Jenny's face. She turned away quickly in order that it might not be seen. Emmy still continued busy with her thoughts. It occurred to her to be surprised that Jenny should be fully dressed. The surprise pressed her further onward with the narrative.

'And, then of course, we found Pa. Wasn't it strange of him to do it? He couldn't have been there long. . . . He must have waited for you to go up. He must have listened. I must find another place to keep it, though he's never done such a thing before in his life. He must have listened for you going up, and then come creeping out here. . . . Why, there's his candle on the floor! Fancy that! Might have set fire to the whole house! See, you couldn't have been upstairs long. . . . I thought you must have been, seeing the fire was black out. Did you go to sleep in front of it? I thought you might have laid a bit of supper for us. I thought you *would* have. But if you were asleep, I don't wonder, I thought you'd have been in bed hours. Did you hear anything? He must have made a racket falling off the chair. What made you come down again? Pa must have listened like anything.'

'I didn't come down,' Jenny said, in a slow, passionless voice. 'I hadn't gone to bed. I was out. I'd been out all the evening . . . since quarter-to-nine.'

IV

At first Emmy could not understand. She stood, puzzled, unable to collect her thoughts.

'Jenny!' at last she said, unbelievingly. Accusing impulses showed in her face. The softer mood, just passing, was replaced by one of anger.

'Well, I must say it's like you,' Emmy concluded. 'I'm not to have a *moment* out of the house. I can't even leave you . . .'

'Half an hour after you'd gone,' urged Jenny, 'I got a note from Keith.'

'Keith!' It was Emmy's sign that she had noted the name.

'I told you. . . . He'd only got the one evening in London.'

'Couldn't he have come here?'

'He mustn't leave his ship. I didn't know what to do. At first I thought I *couldn't* go. But the man was waiting——'

'Man!' cried Emmy. 'What man?'

'The chauffeur.'

Emmy's face changed. Her whole manner changed. She was outraged.

'Jenny! Is he *that* sort! Oh, I warned you. . . . There's never any good in it. He'll do you no good.'

'He's a captain of a little yacht. He's not what you think,' Jenny protested, very pale, her heart sinking under such a rebuke, under such knowledge as she alone possessed.

'Still, to go to him!' Emmy returned to that aspect of the affair. 'And leave Pa!'

'I know. I know,' Jenny cried. She was no longer protective. She was herself in need of comfort. 'But I *had* to go. You'd have gone yourself!' She met Emmy's gaze steadily, but without defiance.

'No I shouldn't!' It was Emmy who became defiant. Emmy's jealousy was again awake. 'However much I wanted to go. I should have stayed.'

'And lost him!' Jenny cried.

'Are you sure of him now?' asked Emmy swiftly. 'If he's gone again.'

With her cheeks crimson, Jenny turned upon her sister.

'Yes, I'm sure of him. And I love him. I love him as much as you love Alf.' She had the impulse, almost irresistible, to add 'More!' but she restrained her tongue just in time. That was a possibility Emmy could never admit. It was only that they were different.

'But to leave Pa!' Emmy's bewildered mind went back to what was the real difficulty. Jenny protested.

'He was in bed. I thought he'd be safe. He was tucked up. Supposing I hadn't gone. Supposing I'd gone up to bed an hour ago. Still he'd have done the same.'

'You know he wouldn't,' Emmy said, very quietly. Jenny felt a wave of hysteria pass through her. It died down. She held herself very firmly. It was true. She knew that she was only defending herself.

'I don't know,' she said, in a false, aggrieved voice. 'How do I know?'

'You do. He knew you were out. He very likely woke up and felt frightened.'

'Felt thirsty, more like it!' Jenny exclaimed.

'Well, you did wrong,' Emmy said. 'However you like to put it to yourself, you did wrong.'

'I always manage to. Don't I!' Jenny's speech still was without defiance. She was humble. 'It's a funny thing; but it's true . . .'

'You always want to go your own way,' Emmy reproved.

'Oh, I don't think *that*'s wrong!' hastily said Jenny. 'Why should you go anybody else's way?'

'I don't know,' admitted Emmy. 'But it's safer.'

'Whose way do you go?' Jenny had stumbled upon a question so unanswerable that she was at liberty to answer it for herself. 'I don't know whose way you go now; but I do know whose way you'll go soon. You'll go Alf's way.'

'Well?' demanded Emmy. 'If it's a good way?'

'Well, I go Keith's way!' Jenny answered, in a fine glow. 'And he goes mine.'

Emmy looked at her, shaking her head in a kind of narrow wisdom.

'Not if he sends a chauffeur,' she said slowly. 'Not that sort of man.'

v

FOR a moment Jenny's heart burned with indignation. Then it turned cold. If Emmy were right! Supposing—just supposing . . . Savagely she thrust doubt of Keith from her: her trust in him was forced by dread into still warmer and louder proclamation.

'You don't understand!' she cried. 'You *couldn't*. You've never seen him. Wait a minute!' She went quickly out of the kitchen and up to her bedroom. There, secretly kept from every eye, was the little photograph of Keith. She brought it down. In anxious triumph she showed it to Emmy. Emmy's three years' seniority had never been of so much account. 'There,' Jenny said. 'That's Keith. Look at him!'

Emmy held the photograph under the meagre light. She was astonished, although she kept outwardly calm; because Keith—besides being obviously what is called a gentleman—looked honest and candid. She could not find fault with the face.

'He's very good-looking,' she admitted, in a critical tone. 'Very.'

'Not the sort of man you thought,' emphasized Jenny, keenly elated at Emmy's dilemma.

'Is he . . . has he got any money?'

'Never asked him. No—I don't think he has. It wasn't *his* chauffeur. A lord's.'

'There! He knows lords. . . . Oh, Jenny!' Emmy's tone was still one of warning. 'He won't marry you. I'm sure he won't.'

'Yes, he will,' Jenny said confidently. But the excitement had shaken her, and she was not the firm Jenny of custom. She looked imploringly at Emmy. '*Say* you believe it!' she begged. Emmy returned her urgent gaze, and felt Jenny's arm round her. Their two faces were very close. 'You'd have done the same,' Jenny urged.

Something in her tone awakened a suspicion in Emmy's mind. She tried to see what lay behind those glowing mysteries that were so close to hers. Her own eyes were shining as if from an inner brightness. The sisters, so unlike, so inexpressibly contrary in every phase of their outlook, in every small detail of their history, had this in common—that each, in her own manner, and with the consequences drawn from differences of character and aim, had spent happy hours with the man she loved. What was to follow remained undetermined. But Emmy's heart was warmed with happiness: she was for the first time filled only with impulses of kindness and love for Jenny. She would blame no more for Jenny's desertion. It was just enough since the consequences of that desertion had been remedied, to enhance Emmy's sense of her own superiority. There remained only the journey taken by Jenny. She again took from her sister's hand the little photograph. Alf's face seemed to come between the photograph and her careful, poring scrutiny, more the jealous scrutiny of a mother than that of a sister.

'He's rather *thin*,' Emmy ventured, dubiously. 'What colour are his eyes?'

'Blue. And his hair's brown. . . . He's lovely.'

'He *looks* nice,' Emmy said, relenting.

'He *is* nice. Em, dear . . . Say you'd have done the same!'

Emmy gave Jenny a great hug, kissing her as if Jenny had been her little girl. To Emmy the moment was without alloy. Her own future assured, all else fell into the orderly picture which made up her view of life. But she was not quite calm, and it even surprised her to feel so much warmth of love for Jenny. Still holding her sister, she was conscious of a quick impulse that was both exulting and pathetically shy.

'It's funny us both being happy at once. Isn't it!' she whispered, all sparkling.

VI

To herself, Jenny groaned a sufficient retort.

'I don't know that I'm feeling so tremendously happy my own self,' she thought. For the re-action had set in. She was glad enough to bring about by various movements their long-delayed bedward journey. She was beginning to feel that her head and her heart were both aching, and that any more confidences from Emmy would be unbearable. And where Emmy had grown communicative—since Emmy had nothing to conceal—Jenny had felt more and more that her happiness was staled as thought corroded it. By the time they turned out the kitchen gas the clock pointed to twenty minutes past two, and the darkest hour was already recorded. In three more hours the sun would rise, and Jenny knew that long before then she would see the sky greying as though the successive veils of the transformation were to reveal the crystal grotto. She preceded Emmy up the stairs, carrying a candle and lighting the way. At the top of the staircase Emmy would find her own candle, and they would part. They were now equally eager for the separation, Emmy because she wanted to think over and over again the details of her happiness, and to make plans for a kind of life that was to open afresh in days that lay ahead. Arrived at the landing the sisters did not pause or kiss, but each looked and smiled seriously as she entered her bedroom. With the closing of the doors noise seemed to depart from the little house, though Jenny heard Emmy moving in her room. The house was in darkness. Emmy was gone; Pa lay asleep in the dim light, his head bandaged and the water slowly soaking into the towel protectively laid upon his chest; in the kitchen the ailing clock ticked away the night. Everything seemed at peace but Jenny, who, when she had closed the door and set her candle down, went quickly to the bed, sitting upon its edge and looking straight before her with dark and sober eyes.

She had much to think of. She would never forgive herself now for leaving Pa. It might have been a more serious accident that had happened

during her absence; she could even plead, to
Emmy, that the accident might have happened
if she had not left the house at all; but nothing
her quick brain could urge had really satisfied
Jenny. The stark fact remained that she had
been there under promise to tend Pa; and that
she had failed in her acknowledged trust. He
might have died. If he had died, she would have
been to blame. Not Pa! He couldn't help himself! He was driven by inner necessity to do
things which he must not be allowed to do.
Jenny might have pleaded the same justification.
She had done so before this. It had been a
necessity to her to go to Keith. As far as that
went she did not question the paramount power
of impulse. Not will, but the strongest craving,
had led her. Jenny could perhaps hardly discourse learnedly upon such things: she must
follow the dictates of her nature. But she never
accused Pa of responsibility. He was an irre-
sponsible. She had been left to look after him.
She had not stayed; and ill had befallen. A
bitter smile curved Jenny's lips.

'I suppose they'd say it was a punishment,'
she whispered. 'They'd like to think it was.'

After that she stayed a long time silent, swaying gently while her candle flickered, her head
full of a kind of formless musing. Then she rose
from the bed and took her candle so that she
could see her face in the small mirror upon the
dressing-table. The candle flickered still more in

the draught from the open window; and Jenny saw her breath hang like a cloud before her. In the mirror her face looked deadly pale; and her lips were slightly drawn as if she were about to cry. Dark shadows were upon her face, whether real or the work of the feeble light she did not think to question. She was looking straight at her own eyes, black with the dilation of pupil, and somehow struck with the horror which was her deepest emotion. Jenny was speaking to the girl in the glass.

'I shouldn't have thought it of you,' she was saying. 'You come out of a respectable home and you do things like this. Silly little fool, you are. Silly little fool. Because you can't stand his not loving you . . . you go and do that.' For a moment she stopped, turning away, her lip bitten, her eyes veiled. 'Oh, but he does love me!' she breathed. '*Quite* as much . . . quite as much . . . nearly . . . nearly as much . . .' She sighed deeply, standing lone in the centre of the room, her long thin shadow thrown upon the wall in front of her. 'And to leave Pa!' she was thinking, and shaking her head. '*That* was wrong, when I'd promised. I shall always know it was wrong. I shall never be able to forget it as long as I live. Not as long as I live. And if I hadn't gone, I'd never have seen Keith again—never! He'd have gone off; and my heart would have broken. I should have got older and older, and hated everybody. Hated Pa, most likely.

And now I just hate myself. . . . Oh, it's so difficult!' She moved impatiently, and at last went
back to the mirror, not to look into it but to
remove the candle, to blow it out, and to leave
the room in darkness. This done, Jenny drew
up the blind, so that she could see the outlines
of the roofs opposite. It seemed to her that for a
long distance there was no sound at all: only
there, all the time, far behind all houses, somewhere buried in the heart of London, there was
the same unintermittent low growl. It was always
in her ears, even at night, like a sleepless pulse,
beating steadily through the silences.

Jenny was not happy. Her heart was cold.
She continued to look from the window, her face
full of gravity. She was hearing again Keith's
voice as he planned their future; but she was not
sanguine now. It all seemed too far away, and
so much had happened. So much had happened
that seemed as though it could never be realised,
never be a part of memory at all, so blank and
sheer did it now stand, pressing upon her like
overwhelming darkness. She thought again of
the bridge, and the striking hours; the knock, the
letter, the hurried ride; she remembered her
supper and the argument with Emmy; the argument with Alf; and her fleeting moods, so many,
so painful, during her time with Keith. To love,
to be loved: that was her sole commandment of
life—how learned she knew not. To love and to
work she knew was the theory of Emmy. But

how different they were, how altogether unlike!
Emmy with Alf; Jenny with Keith . . .

'Yes, but she's got what she wants,' Jenny whispered in the darkness. 'That's what she wants.
It wouldn't do for me. Only in this world you've
all got to have one pattern, whether it suits you
or not. Else you're not "right." "They" don't
like it. And I'm outside . . . I'm a misfit. Eh,
well: it's no good whimpering about it. What
must be, must; as they say!'

Soberly she moved from the window and
began to undress in the darkness, stopping
every now and then as if she were listening
to that low humming far beyond the houses,
when the thought of unresting life made her
heart beat more quickly. Away there upon the
black running current of the river was Keith,
on that tiny yacht so open upon the treacherous
sea to every kind of danger. And nothing between Keith and sudden horrible death but that
wooden hulk and his own seamanship. She was
Keith's: she belonged to him; but he did not
belong to her. To Keith she might, she would
give all, as she had done; but he would still be
apart from her. He might give his love, his care:
but she knew that her pride and her love must
be the love and pride to submit—not Keith's.
Away from him, released from the spell, Jenny
knew that she had yielded to him the freedom she
so cherished as her inalienable right. She had
given him her freedom. It was in his power.

For her real freedom was her innocence and her desire to do right. It was not that she wanted to defy, so much as that she could bear no shackles, and that she had no respect for the belief that things should be done only because they were always done, and for no other reason but that of tradition. And she feared nothing but her own merciless judgment.

It was not now that she dreaded Emmy's powerlessness to forgive her, or the opinion of anybody else in the world. It was that she could not forgive herself. Those who are strong enough to live alone in the world, so long as they are young and vigorous, have this rare faculty of self-judgment. It is only when they are exhausted that they turn elsewhere for judgment and pardon.

Jenny sat once again upon the bed.

'Oh Keith, my dearest . . .' she began. 'My Keith . . .' Her thoughts flew swiftly to the yacht, to Keith. With unforgettable pain she heard his voice ringing in her ears, saw his clear eyes, as honest as the day, looking straight into her own. Pain mingled with love and pride; and battled there within her heart, making a fine tumult of sensation; and Jenny felt herself smiling in the darkness at such a conflict. She even began very softly to laugh. But as if the sound checked her and awoke the secret sadness that the tumultuous sensations were trying to hide, her courage suddenly gave way.

'Keith!' she gently called, her voice barely audible. Only silence was there. Keith was far away—unreachable. Jenny pressed her hands to her lips, that were trembling uncontrollably. She rose, struggling for composure, struggling to get back to the old way of looking at everything. It seemed imperative that she should do so. In a forlorn, quivering voice she ventured:

'What a life! Golly, what a life!'

But the effort to pretend that she could still make fun of the events of the evening was too great for Jenny. She threw herself upon the bed, burying her face in the pillow.

'Keith . . . oh Keith! . . .'